The Tomorrow People *in*
The Visitor

Based on the Thames Television Series

Also available in this series

Julian R. Gregory
and Roger Price

The Tomorrow People *in* THE VISITOR

illustrated by Mike Jackson

Piccolo TV Times Original

First published 1973 by Pan Books Ltd,
Cavaye Place, London SW10 9PG
in association with
Independent Television Publications Ltd,
publishers of *TV Times* and *Look-in*
5th printing 1979
© Roger Price 1973
ISBN 0 330 23477 3
Set, printed and bound in Great Britain by
Cox & Wyman Ltd, London, Reading and Fakenham

Introduction

Their names are John, Stephen, Carol and Kenny. They seem to be just ordinary kids. A bit quieter than most, perhaps. But they are The Tomorrow People, forerunners of a new race, *homo superior*. Gifted with superhuman powers they are Nature's response to man's aggression: a new species, wiser and more peaceloving than *homo sapiens*, and until more of their race evolve these four have intergalactic responsibility for the future of Planet Earth.

In this new adventure an alien child's panic and British governmental ignorance combine to create a situation where one wrong move will mean the destruction of Earth. Only The Tomorrow People know what to do. But will they be allowed to take command?

CHAPTER ONE

Stephen was the first to see it: a long, luminous streak, high in the evening sky. On the ground it was already dark, but the last rays of the sun crept round the curve of the Earth's surface, giving a pink glow to the object hurtling on the edge of space.

Stephen's mind went into overdrive, calculating from the height of the sun's rays the altitude of the object and then working out its speed.

'A hundred thousand kilometres an hour, and decelerating 28g,' he told himself, 'but not burning up. If it's a space-ship, it certainly isn't a Sap one.'

The others had seen it too. Carol's thoughts came in from the top of a bus three miles away. Then came Kenny, then John, all in an excited rush:

'Did you see it, Stephen?'

'It was a space-ship definitely . . .'

1

'It couldn't have been a Sap one.'

'Where do you reckon it came from?'

The object was out of sight now; it had disappeared to the north, over the trees in the park. To the man on the other side of the road, walking his dog, Stephen looked like an ordinary boy, striding morosely along with his hands in his pockets. Not a word of the telepathic conversation buzzing between the Tomorrow People had been picked up by any of the Saps around.

Malcolm Neilson, the doctor's son, ran across from the garden where he had been playing cricket with his young brother. He and Stephen were in the same class at school.

'Hold on a minute,' Stephen sent to the others, 'I've got a Sap to attend to.'

Malcolm was breathless with excitement. His eyes glinted eagerly behind his large spectacles.

'Did you see that, Stephen?'

'Yes,' said Stephen.

'What was it? Do you reckon it was a UFO?'

'It was probably just a satellite – Russian or American – burning up as it re-entered the atmosphere.' Stephen spoke with the air of someone who thought the subject of little significance. Then he immediately began to wonder if he wasn't overdoing it in his attempt to appear ignorant and ordinary.

'Perhaps it was a meteorite.' Malcolm ventured. 'It *was* a meteorite, I bet you anything.'

'If it was,' said Stephen, 'we'd have heard the bang by now. It must have been the biggest in history.'

Malcolm gave a snort and turned back towards his

brother, who was tagging along dragging the cricket bat.

Stephen hoped he hadn't been too offhand. When he was relaxed he found it fairly easy to live like a Sap, but when he had other things on his mind, he sometimes found it difficult to seem natural and ordinary. He wondered about all the other youngsters he could see through the park railings, kicking balls about, scrambling, tumbling, fighting. Were they all going to 'break out' one day and become Tomorrow People? It seemed impossible; yet, it had happened to him and it would almost certainly happen to some of them. Perhaps even to Malcolm. You never knew . . .

When he got home five minutes later, a Newscaster on the TV set in the living-room was busy telling the nation that a giant meteorite had just passed across the sky. 'That'll make Malcolm's day,' he thought.

At the same time, he felt concern. Of course, the object could not possibly have been a meteorite. Not even Sap scientists would be stupid enough to think that it was.

It followed that the Government was deliberately lying, in order to keep the real truth secret. But why? The Tomorrow People had to find out.

'Was it a meteorite?' asked his father from the armchair. Along with the other parents of the Tomorrow People Stephen's Dad knew what his son was, even if he could never fully comprehend what it involved. 'No, Dad,' Stephen replied. 'What it was we don't know. But it wasn't a meteorite.'

3

John burst through with a message: 'Did you see that rubbish on the box?'

Stephen's father watched his son in silent communion with his distant friend.

'Why do you think they're putting it out?' asked John.

'So people won't panic, I reckon,' put in Carol. 'They've made up their minds it's a space-ship. And for my money, they're right.'

'Has it landed?' asked John.

'I haven't checked with TIM yet,' said Stephen. 'I've only just got in.'

'I'll bet it has,' chimed in Kenny from his home in the East End.

'We'd better get cracking,' said John impatiently.

Stephen took a tiny, spherical communicator from his pocket and touched it to his forehead. The calm unruffled voice of TIM flooded into his brain.

From his home in the Tomorrow People's secret headquarters, deep below the London streets, the computer gave Stephen the fundamental data on the object: speed, trajectory and spectroscopic analysis. Stephen's estimate of the first two had been correct. The third mystified him. He needed to know much more, though he now felt certain that the object was a space-ship.

Switching to speech, he told his father: 'I'm going to jaunt, Dad – only to the Lab, so don't worry.'

It was a kindly warning. For Stephen's father, the sight of his son suddenly disappearing into thin air was still an unnerving experience. To tell the truth, Stephen had hardly got used to the miracle of teleportation himself, although it was more than a year since he had

4

'broken out'. Their own name for it was 'jaunting', a word they had borrowed from a science fiction story.

It was a simple process, to think oneself out of existence in one place, pass briefly through hyperspace, and enter existence in another place a fifth of a second later. Once a Tomorrow Person had mastered the technique it was easy. For most journeys, the belt was necessary: not to make jaunting possible, but merely as a navigational aid. Without the belts, if the jaunter wasn't absolutely certain where he was going, he might materialize in outer space, or in a block of concrete, or deep in the magma of the Earth's crust . . .

Stephen knew exactly where he was going, but the jaunt was electrifying, as always. He caught a brief glimpse of his own body, hazing as it dematerialized. For that fifth of a second he saw the swirling nothingness of hyperspace. Then he stood in front of TIM.

'You came without using your belt again,' TIM pointed out gently. 'I keep telling you, it could be dangerous.'

'I like to do things myself,' replied Stephen.

On his videoscreen, TIM began to pour out all the data which he had amassed since the space-ship came within range of the observer satellite. It had come from deep space, at a speed much faster than light. But from where?

The trigonometrical reading gave little indication. Possibly from somewhere in Andromeda; but so far as they knew there was no space-travelling civilization in that galaxy. It was more probable that the ship had come from a planet infinitely further away.

The spectroscopic reading, which TIM now showed

him again on the videoscreen, was even more puzzling. Whatever kind of substance the spaceship was made of, Stephen had never encountered it before. It certainly did not exist on any of the planets the Tomorrow People had visited.

'Not much to go on, TIM,' he frowned. 'That's all you got from the satellite?'

'The satellite was on the far side of its orbit when the space-ship came in,' said TIM. 'As you can see, the ship was only travelling at slightly less than the speed of light when it entered the Earth's atmosphere.'

'Yes, its deceleration was fantastic,' Stephen replied. 'Even I noticed that, from the ground.'

The headquarters were in a disused tunnel of the London underground. The tunnel was to have formed part of the Victoria Line, but the engineers had hit a geological fault and work had been abandoned. All that had been many years ago, and few of the millions of Londoners knew that the tunnel existed, still less what it housed. Officially, all entrances had been bricked up; in fact, one tiny door remained open, known only to the Tomorrow People.

It was TIM, of course, who dominated the cavernous laboratory. Close to him stood the teleporter – the large jaunting-vehicle which could transmit the Tomorrow People and their equipment to any corner of the universe, just as swiftly as Stephen had come here from his own sitting-room.

Around the walls were stacked memory-erasers and paralysing pistols, or 'stun guns' – weapons with which to deal harmlessly with the dangerous enemies who might, at any moment, confront them on their travels. In addition, there were the ordinary instruments of their work: communicators, which enabled them to talk to TIM telepathically; electro-scanners, and jaunting-belts. Some of the newer gadgets – the electro-scanner, for example – Stephen had designed himself, to the delight of his companions. His mechanical gifts had become an enormous asset to the Tomorrow People, when he finally broke out, at the age of thirteen, and became the latest of their number.

CHAPTER TWO

So far there were four of them – John, Carol, Stephen and Kenny. Although Carol now realized that 'breaking out' was the most wonderful thing that could happen to anyone, she still could not look back on the experience without a shudder.

She was playing rounders in the park; it was a hot August afternoon at the height of the school holiday, and several of her friends had already drifted towards the soft-drink stall beside the main gate. She, too, was beginning to think longingly of orangeade when, without warning, the noises began inside her head.

Noises, but not the sort of noises anyone besides herself could hear. In fact, as she now knew, they were thoughts – hundreds of thousands of thoughts, from hundreds of thousands of heads in the city all around her, flooding into her brain and deafening her with their wild, mixed-up clamour. So acute were they that she thought she would go out of her mind – drowning in a sea of other people's hopes and fears, plans and memories. As John put it, it was just like having the world's biggest football stadium, right there inside your head.

Completely paralysed with fear, she ignored a call to run for base and collapsed on the ground screaming, her hands pressed to her head. She remembered clearly the anxious faces of her friends as they gathered round her: the face of the park-keeper, grave and bewildered; the face of the young woman doctor, pretty in her white tennis-frock, who had hurried across from the nearby courts. Fresh from medical school, she had proved almost helpless; she could only try, ineffectively, to make Carol comfortable until the ambulance arrived . .

When Carol came round, four hours later, she was in a private nursing-home. The voices in her head were still there, but they were now muffled and no longer disturbed her.

A new face looked down at her. It belonged to a tall, broad-shouldered man with horn-rimmed spectacles and a small, silver beard. Behind him, in a respectful semi-circle, stood a group of doctors and nurses, each of whom called him 'sir'. He looked extremely wise, extremely kind, and extremely puzzled – although, Carol sensed, he was trying not to show it. Phrases in a foreign accent floated – 'catatonic trance' . . . 'traumatic shock' . . 'slowly reduce the degree of sedation'.

Seeing that Carol had recovered consciousness, he smiled at her: 'No doubt, in a day or two, she will explain what occasioned this shock and we shall all be a great deal wiser.'

Everyone else smiled too, and the great man went on his way. But when Carol left the nursing-home, two days later, she had told nobody about the noises in her head. First, because she did not think that anyone would believe her; secondly, because she had heard from John who had 'broken out' three months earlier.

As soon as she came out of her trance he sent out comforting thought-messages, assuring her that all was well, that she was on the threshold of an exciting adventure. She had suddenly developed, he told her, a rare and mysterious gift; a gift which belonged, for the present at least, only to the two of them.

The next person to break out was Kenny, the cheery little West African cockney. He was only eleven, and he had suffered a greater shock than any of them; in TIM's view. Nature had erred in allowing him to break out while he was still so young. Carol had been thirteen and John fourteen, and it had been hard enough for them.

But for the help which they were able to give him, Kenny might never have recovered from his trance. Now, two years later, he was more buoyant, more full of fun, than all the others put together.

As he pored over the figures which TIM had given to him, Stephen could hear Kenny's excited questions bouncing through the miles which separated them. Where had the space-ship come from? Where was it now? Why had it come to Earth? Were there Tomorrow People inside it?

'If you shut up for a minute, I might be able to tell

11

you,' Stephen replied tetchily. 'At least, we should know where it has landed.'

He finished his calculations and fed the results back into TIM. At once, TIM produced the answer.

'Scotland, just as I thought,' he said.

TIM had pin-pointed a spot on the west coast, about twenty miles north of Oban.

'We went to Oban for our holidays last year,' Carol told him.

'What's this place called?'

'Kilgardie,' Stephen replied. 'According to TIM it's not on any of the maps – at least, not on the big ones. I bet it's wondering what hit it.'

'Aren't we all,' put in John. 'I suggest we don't waste any time. Let's jaunt over there now and find out.'

Within minutes, they were all beside Stephen in the underground headquarters, having paused only long enough to tell their parents that they were off on another mission. Their parents, in turn, had sighed resignedly, urged them to be careful and then gone about the ordinary business of the evening, trying not to imagine where their offspring might be – or what they might be up to.

Stephen's father, now attempting once more to concentrate on his newspaper, was a physicist employed on medical research at one of the great London hospitals. Though he was extremely able in his own field, Stephen had soon been forced to give up his attempts to explain to him the mechanics of jaunting and tele-kinesis, the power of moving objects by thought, which all the Tomorrow People possessed. They were simply beyond even the keenest Sap brain. His father had come originally from Scotland and Stephen wondered if it might console him if he knew that his son's latest adventure was taking him there.

Carol lived in Hampstead, with her parents and two younger sisters. Her father, a producer of television documentaries, longed to do a programme about the Tomorrow People but accepted the fact that it would never be possible. Her mother, a journalist, also chafed at having the most sensational story of the century there in her home, when she could not breathe a word about it.

John, the eldest of the Tomorrow People and their unofficial leader, lived in North London, where his father was a police sergeant. Kenny's father had died when he was very small. He and his sister lived with their mother, a hospital sister who had come from West Africa as a teenager to begin her training as a nurse.

Each of the Tomorrow People had brought camping gear – tents, groundsheets and sleeping-bags. John had an extra bag for Stephen. It was John who had decided that they had better go disguised as campers. By now, he reckoned, the place would be crawling with Saps – Saps on the look-out for anyone or anything out of place in that isolated spot. The arrival of four youngsters of assorted ages might attract their attention; it would be less likely to do so if they were obviously on holiday. Fortunately, it was still early in September, and in many places the school year had not yet begun.

Swiftly, they stowed their equipment into the teleporter – a shining, rectangular cage with a complex control-panel. Then they filed in, one by one – Carol first, John last of all.

'Right, TIM. We're off,' called John.

'Good luck,' replied TIM. 'Keep in touch.'

Deftly, TIM programmed the controls, co-ordinating the instruments with superhuman precision as he set the course for their destination. No human being could perform this task; even a Tomorrow Person would need years to do the calculations. A single error might bring them out in the middle of Africa – or even on another planet. When TIM signalled that all was ready, John turned to the others.

'All set?' he inquired.

They murmured their assent.

John pushed the starter-button on the panel before him.

In a split second they had landed in Kilgardie.

CHAPTER THREE

It was even smaller than they had imagined – little more than a main street, with a stone kirk at one end, a pub at the other, and a few squat cottages in between.

They had emerged on a hill above the village. Behind them loomed the great peaks of the Highlands, purple with heather in the waning sunlight. To the left beyond the village, one or two crofters' cottages dotted the fields which lay between the mountains and the sea. To the right was a small headland and before them lay the sea itself, empty now save for a small boat – possibly a fishing-boat – in the far distance.

'Nothing here, is there?' said Kenny, ruefully. 'Maybe TIM has slipped up.'

'TIM never slips up,' answered John, curtly. 'If he says the ship landed here, then it landed here.'

Calling on the others to follow him, he scrambled

down the hillside, his rucksack bouncing on his back. The others followed, Carol keeping a guiding hand on Kenny as they half walked and half slithered to the road below. They could, of course, have jaunted down, but they had no wish to attract unwelcome attention.

They set off up the street without meeting a soul. Several of the cottage doors were open, but it was clear that there was no one inside, although fires were burning and television and radio sets left on. It looked as though the entire village had suddenly deserted the fireside and the tea-table and gone – where?

John looked out to sea once more. The water seemed calm and unruffled; the tide was going out and scarcely a ripple broke on the shore below. In the distance, the sail of the fishing-boat seemed to have grown larger. No doubt, thought John, he was making for home before darkness fell. Perhaps when he did put in he'd be able to explain the mystery.

The four stopped outside the door of the pub. John paused. He'd never been inside a pub before, but he knew that here, if anywhere, he ought to find somebody.

He pushed the door gently, and stepped into the little bar.

Here, too, it was obvious that everyone had suddenly jumped up and left. Half-finished pint pots and whisky-glasses stood on the tables; behind the gleaming pumps only a twittering budgie kept watch over the deserted room.

John stepped outside.

'Empty, like everywhere else,' he told the others. 'They've even left their whisky behind.'

16

'Gosh, I wonder if we've landed in Scotland,' said Stephen with a grin. 'Real Scotsmen would never leave their Scotch.'

Carol pointed out to sea. 'I thought that boat was coming this way,' she said. 'It looks as though it's changing direction.'

She was right. The boat had now veered round and was heading for a point further up the coast on the other side of the headland.

At that moment, an engine whined in the distance: an aero-engine, coming rapidly nearer. Soon, a helicopter appeared over the mountains behind them, then another. With a frightening clatter they swept low overhead, then touched down, out of sight, on the sea-shore beyond the headland.

'Come on,' said John.

'Jaunt?' said Carol.

'Not likely,' said John. 'We're going to find a lot of very frightened people on the other side of there. Think of the reaction if we appeared from nowhere!'

Stepping out briskly along the narrow coast road, they rounded the headland as still more helicopters came in to land.

In a tight group on the sea-shore stood the villagers, men, women and children. Altogether there were about forty of them, huddled together as though for re-assurance – though against what, nobody knew. Two police cars had drawn up on the coast road behind them. A young constable and a sergeant, notebooks poised, were taking statements from some of the men and, by the look of it, having a hard time in getting a coherent picture.

Further down the beach, a senior police officer was conferring gravely with two army officers – one middle-aged, the other younger – who had landed in the first helicopter. As he spoke, he pointed to the sea, which still appeared calm and unruffled. A number of other soldiers had strung themselves out along the sand. They gave the villagers friendly grins, as though to put them at their ease. But John could see that they were tense, alert – as though waiting for orders which they knew might be difficult and dangerous beyond anything they had ever experienced.

Behind them, nearer to the water's edge, still more troops were disembarking from the newly-arrived choppers.

John turned to the others.

'Right,' he said. 'Remember, we arrived today on the train from London. We got off at Inverness and we have hitch-hiked the rest.'

'What, all four of us?' said Kenny.

'A farmer gave us a lift in his Land-Rover,' said John. 'But only if anyone asks.'

Wearing expressions of naïve curiosity, they walked slowly towards the group on the beach. The police sergeant turned as they approached.

'Hello – and who might you be?' he demanded. They told their story.

'And did you see anything – anything strange?' said the sergeant, cautiously.

'No,' replied John, the spokesman. 'We saw the helicopters and we've just come to see what's happening.'

'That's what we'd all like to know,' the sergeant observed.

At that moment, the superintendent – John could now see that he was a superintendent – walked up.

'Are these youngsters from the village?' he asked the sergeant curtly.

'No, sir. Campers, from London,' the sergeant replied.

The superintendent looked at them carefully for a moment. John thought he was about to ask more questions. Instead he turned back to the sergeant.

'All right,' he said. 'Get them out of here. All these people as well. The military want the place clear.'

'Very good, sir,' said the sergeant. He turned back to the Tomorrow People.

'You heard that, young friends,' he said. 'Back you go, the way you came.'

As they turned to go, he called after them kindly: 'If you want a spot to camp in, speak nicely to Mr McCaig over there. Perhaps he'll find you a corner in one of his fields.'

A crofter of fifty, with a weatherbeaten face, turned to look at them out of steel-blue eyes. Clearly, he was still recovering from the shock which he and his neighbours had received, and it took him a moment to focus his attention on the four Tomorrow People.

Finally, he nodded. 'Aye,' he said. 'Aye, ye can camp on my land, certainly. Come along.'

They fell into step beside him, as the police shepherded all the villagers back along the coast road. Behind them the fishing-boat had moved in close to the shore and one of the army officers was directing it away through a loud-hailer.

'What happened, sir?' John asked him, after they had introduced themselves.

Mr McCaig paused before he replied.

'Something went into the sea,' he said. 'No more than a mile out. Something that came out of the sky.'

'A meteorite?' Stephen suggested.

'That's what they are saying,' replied Mr McCaig. 'But . . .'

He stopped, as though wondering whether he should say any more.

'Yes, sir?' said John.

The crofter looked at him warily, his eyes shining in his deep, lined face.

'I saw it, laddie,' he said. 'I and some of the others, too. And if that was a meteorite, it was no like anything any of us had ever imagined.'

'What *was* it like?' asked Kenny, innocently.

Once again there was a long pause before the answer came.

'It was green,' said Mr McCaig. 'Green and shining . . . shining from within, like the neon signs you have in the city. It was shaped like a cigar – no, maybe more like a pencil, pointed at the nose.'

'How long was it?' asked Carol.

'Fifty feet, maybe,' replied the crofter.

'You seem to have got a good look at it,' John observed.

'Aye, I did,' said Mr McCaig. 'And so did the others.'

He stopped yet again, as though fearing that they might not believe him.

'You see, before it finally sank into the sea, it stopped.'

'Stopped?' asked Kenny.

'Hovered, you might say. In mid-air, just like a kestrel. Then it just sank, gently. It hardly made a ripple.'

The Tomorrow People looked at one another. The description which their host had given did not fit any space-ship which they had yet come across. They wondered who might be in the ship and what would happen if the military managed to locate it.

To Mr McCaig the youngsters appeared silent. In fact, they were having an urgent telepathic discussion. Supposing that the ship had come to Earth on a mission, said John, it was vitally important that they should reach it first and, if possible, make friendly contact with the occupants. Soldiers were trained to regard all invaders as enemies and that meant that, faced with visitors from outer space, they might shoot first and ask questions afterwards. And that could be fatal, perhaps fatal for the whole Earth . . .

They had reached Mr McCaig's croft; it was one of those which they had noticed when they first landed, at the opposite end of the village from the headland. His wife joined them, a small, grey-haired woman with a gentle manner. She had, it turned out, walked back behind them with some of the other women.

'You'll come in for tea first,' she said. 'There'll be time to pitch your tents afterwards, before it goes dark. My husband will show you where.'

They began to protest that they could not impose on her, but she brushed their objections aside with a wave.

'You can't bed down on empty stomachs,' she said.

21

'And you won't get a hot meal anywhere round here at this time of night.'

Had they not been so preoccupied, they might have enjoyed the great platefuls of bacon and fried potatoes which she set before them, and the beautifully baked apple pie which followed. As it was, their minds constantly veered towards the ship lying below the waves, and throughout the meal they tried repeatedly to make telepathic contact with whoever might be inside. Unfortunately, Mrs McCaig noticed their silence.

'I must say, you're the quietest bunch of youngsters I've ever met,' she declared. 'But no doubt you're tired after your long journey.'

After they had thanked her sincerely for the meal, her husband showed them out to a sheltered corner of the field beyond the cottage, and left them to put up their tents. Out beyond the headland naval patrol-boats were now circling the spot where the space-ship had disappeared and already, in the dusk, searchlights were sweeping the water.

'What do we do now?' Kenny asked.

'For the moment – nothing,' replied John. 'There's nothing we can do.'

If there were people in the space-ship, he reasoned, they were plainly from a civilization much more scientifically advanced than our own and almost certainly possessed the power to free themselves. If, on the other hand, they could not live under water, they were already dead. There was, of course, a third possibility – that the ship was unmanned. If that were so, they were still left with the question of why had it been sent to Earth.

Each of them, even Kenny, felt, more keenly than ever before, what it meant to be a Tomorrow Person. The responsibility was truly enormous. The lives of countless people all over the globe might well depend on their making the right decision during the next twenty-four hours.

At first, Carol and John had not realized the full significance of breaking out. It was only as their powers began to develop, in particular, as they found themselves able to visit distant corners of the universe, that they learned the truth about themselves.

On a planet called Sophia, in the galactic arm of Perseus, there lived an immortal race of philosophers who had invited them to jaunt there soon after Kenny joined their number. It was the Sophists who explained to them that they were the first people on Earth to reach a new level of evolution. Nature, fearful that mankind would destroy itself, had speeded up the evolutionary process and produced a new species, *homo superior*, who would take over the Earth and turn it into a planet in which technology would be used only in the cause of peace and wars would be unknown. After that visit the four had built TIM, to a design which the Sophists had given to them.

When the three returned to Earth, they had wondered what to call themselves. *Homo superior* sounded ... well, too superior. It was John who found the name that they all agreed was perfect – the Tomorrow People. Now they were waiting for others to join them. That there would be more, they were quite certain; the Sophists had promised them that. But who they were, or where they were, the Tomorrow People had no way of knowing. Nobody could tell whether a youngster was a Tomorrow Person, until he or she broke out.

As she settled herself to sleep, Carol wondered how many of them there were, and how long it would be before they could take over from the Saps . . .

CHAPTER FOUR

She awoke in the darkness with a scream, struggling out of her sleeping-bag and clutching at the empty air. At first, she thought that she had been having a nightmare, and then, as she became more fully awake, that she had walked in her sleep, out across the beach and into the sea.

She felt wet and frightened – more frightened than ever in her life. She had just come out of the sea and she was being dragged up the beach to the road, struggling in vain to free herself from the hands which held her. Looking up, she could see that she was being gripped by two large soldiers: they might easily have been two of those who had emerged from the helicopters earlier in the evening. For an instant, the vision was so strong that she knew that it must be real; that it could be no dream. Then, in a split second, it was gone. She was alone in her tent, sobbing.

25

Sounds came from the other tents. Her cries must have roused the others and she only hoped that she had not disturbed the McCaigs. Then, as she struggled out of the tent, she realized that nobody was coming to find out what was wrong with her. Instead, each of the boys was crying out in fear, just as she had done.

Pushing into the tent which Stephen shared with Kenny, she shook both of them. Instantly, they stopped yelling and looked at her, as though seeing her for the first time. Kenny was still whimpering gently.

In a second John appeared at her side. He, too, looked shaken in the moonlight.

As they pulled themselves together John glanced across to the cottage, expecting at any moment to see the light go on. But it remained in darkness. Fortunately, the McCaigs were sound sleepers.

Each of them had had exactly the same experience. Each had imagined that he was being pulled from the sea and across the beach by the military. Kenny thought that they were about to bundle him into a helicopter.

John put a finger to his lips. 'Listen!' he told the others.

In the distance, beyond the headland, an engine roared. In a second a helicopter rose from the beach, its lights clearly visible in the darkness, and clattered off over the mountains, disturbing flocks of sleeping birds.

In one or two of the houses in the village bedroom lights went on as the people inside came to their windows to find out what had disturbed them. Seeing the helicopter they muttered darkly and stumbled back to bed.

'If all four of us had the same experience, it couldn't have been a nightmare,' said John. 'We never send messages in our dreams – at least, we never have done yet. So I don't see that one of us could have dreamed it and transmitted it to the rest.'

'What was it then?' asked Carol.

'I think I can guess,' said John. 'We each received a strong visual image which was sent from an outside source.'

'You mean, somebody from the space-ship was calling to us?' asked Stephen.

'Calling to anybody within range,' replied John. 'Anybody capable of picking up a telepathic signal.'

'But this wasn't like any signal I've ever received before,' said Stephen. 'I mean . . . it was entirely visual. There were no words, no attempt to say what was wrong. Whoever he is, he just made us see out of his eyes for a few seconds.'

'And feel what he was feeling,' added Carol with a shudder. 'Next time he gets the wind up, I hope I'm not too much within range. I don't want another shock like that in a hurry.'

'It seems as though this individual, whoever he is, has not reached a very high degree of development,' said John.

'Not highly developed? How do you mean?' asked Carol, puzzled.

'I mean that he can only say what he sees or what he feels in the simplest possible way,' John told her. 'For a telepathic being, that means making someone else see it or feel it.'

'But he landed here in a superluminary space-ship,'

Stephen objected. 'He can hardly be so simple as all that if he can travel faster than light.'

'He also landed in the sea and allowed himself to be caught within a few hours,' John pointed out evenly. 'Neither of these actions indicate any high degree of intelligence – what's more, it would seem that he is totally unable to jaunt.'

'Whoever he is, the army have got him now,' Kenny put in. 'And we have got to find him – quick.'

John used his communicator to call up TIM and ask him where the military would be most likely to take the visitor from outer space.

'There is a medical research establishment, controlled by the Ministry of Defence, twenty miles due east of where you are now,' TIM told them. 'It is surrounded by mountains and stands on the shores of a small lake called Loch Derrig.'

The four grinned at each other. They each felt a surge of hope and excitement, even though they knew that danger lay ahead.

'Thank you, TIM,' John said, before flicking off his communicator.

'Good luck,' responded TIM.

John looked round at the others.

'Ready?' he asked.

'Ready,' they replied.

TIM, by remote control, had already set their belts.

'Right,' said John. 'Jaunt!'

Once again they landed on a hillside. There were still several hours to dawn and the silence around them seemed eerie; their ears missed the gentle wash of the sea. The moon, reflected in the loch below, showed them the peaks rising like witches' teeth on all sides. Here and there the surface of the mountainside showed darker as a pine-forest struggled up the slope.

At first, they could see no sign of the medical centre, nor any other sign of life. Once again, Kenny began to wonder whether TIM had misdirected them. This time, however, he kept his doubts to himself.

It was John who spotted the buildings, his eyes grown accustomed to this new and deeper darkness. Immediately below them, hard against the loch shore, lay a collection of flat roofs. Most were long, single-storey buildings, but one was taller: it had at least two storeys and possibly three.

Slowly, they descended towards the centre, their eyes straining for any sign of movement. Surely, thought John, the place must be in a flurry of activity; everyone down there must know by now that they were about to receive the army's first captive from another planet. Yet they could see no indication that the place was inhabited at all.

As they reached the bottom of the slope, a barbed-wire fence rose before them. No sooner had they seen it, than there was a loud rustle at the side. They froze, hands on belts, ready to jaunt. Small feet pattered away through the darkness, and four sighs of relief rose towards the moon. They had disturbed a sleeping animal: a hare, perhaps, or a stoat. In the distance, an owl hooted.

John motioned to the others to gather round.

'First we reconnoitre,' he said. 'When we know the

layout of the place, and where they are going to keep him, we can decide what to do next.'

As he spoke, a sharp beam of light stabbed the air, then another, then four more. Above them, the roof of the tall building was suddenly a blaze of light and the other buildings were dappled with light and darkness. On the roof and on the ground, men were hurrying. There was no panic, but again there was the tension which they had noticed on the beach at Kilgardie.

'Quick down!' hissed John.

They pressed themselves to the ground, hearts pounding. For a split second Carol feared that they had been spotted, that this was the start of a hue and cry. Then, in the distance, she heard the now-familiar sound of a helicopter engine, and in a few seconds the machine had come clattering over the peaks, throwing all the sleeping wild life into a panic.

They had, of course, arrived ahead of the captors and their prisoner and now they were to see him brought in. Lights blazing, the helicopter eased itself into position over the floodlit roof and then, hovering for a moment, touched gently down.

John made a small sound of disappointment.

'The door's on the other side,' he muttered. 'It looks as though we won't be able to see what he's like.'

He proved to be right. They glimpsed little more than the feet of the soldiers as they alighted on the far side of the helicopter. They came fully into view only for a brief moment as they descended through a huge trap-door in the roof. In that time, they were just able to see a dark figure, half-propelled and half-carried, between two soldiers.

'Gosh,' said Stephen. 'He doesn't look very big.'

Carol, straining after the prisoner as he disappeared, guessed that he was even smaller than Kenny.

In the upper storey of the centre lights had flashed on. A moment later the floodlights on the roof went off, leaving the helicopter silent and in darkness.

'At least we know where they are keeping him,' said Stephen.

'Yes,' said John. 'The problem now is – how do we get him out?'

How indeed? It would, of course, be a straightforward matter to jaunt into the laboratory where the visitor had been taken and snatch him from under the noses of his captors. Stephen fingered the stun gun at his waist. He flattered himself that he was quick enough on the draw to deal with any Sap marksman armed with a conventional army Browning pistol.

The soldiers, he was confident, would not readily shoot down a schoolboy, no matter how much his sudden appearance had taken them by surprise. While they were gathering their wits together, he could paralyse the lot of them with a few quick squirts, then they would jaunt away over the mountains. A touch with the memory-eraser would make sure that the men remembered nothing of what had happened.

It was a splendid idea but, as Stephen himself realized, it was open to one major objection. They did not know yet whether the visitor could jaunt.

If he couldn't, then the whole scheme was a useless dream. In order to get away they would have to use their stun guns to shoot their way out on foot, and that was a plan fraught with dangers which they dare not risk. If only one member of the staff saw them go and was able to tell the tale afterwards the whole country would soon be too hot to hold them. Every army camp and police station in the country would have their description within twenty-four hours.

The dilemma was part of the constant problem which the Tomorrow People had to face at every moment of their lives. Always they had to be on their guard in case they should make some tiny slip and expose themselves to the Saps.

They knew that if they were ever discovered, they would be in the gravest danger from Sap governments and other powerful interests who could not bear the thought that the world was soon to be taken over by a race of Super kids. Their lives would almost certainly be snuffed out and Nature's bold experiment doomed to failure – at least for the time being.

Not for ever, though; for more Tomorrow People would break out, no matter what the Saps did. Only by destroying the world could they prevent the new era that was coming – and the four were determined to see that they didn't do that.

The term 'Sap', which they coined soon after they had broken out, was not meant to be insulting – just short for *homo sapiens*. But there were times when Stephen, especially, thought that the description fitted – and this was one of them. As he glared impotently at the lighted windows of the centre, he muttered it to himself – Saps! It had a comforting sound.

Kenny, kneeling beside him in the darkness, had also been thinking about a snatch.

'Do you think the space-man can jaunt?' he asked.

'If he can, surely he'd have done it by now,' said Carol. 'Maybe we'd better see what TIM thinks.'

John paused. 'Perhaps he can tell us himself – I'll just have one more shot at contacting him,' he said.

'Well, be careful,' said Carol, alarmed. 'Remember what happened when we picked up his distress-signal.'

John chuckled. 'Don't worry,' he said. 'We're prepared, this time.'

Focusing on the small, frightened figure inside the centre, he called, 'We are friends. We have come to rescue you. Can you jaunt?'

And that was the last thing any of them remembered.

CHAPTER FIVE

John was the first to recover consciousness. The sun, streaming in through the window in front of him, blinded him for a moment as he opened his eyes. Before he had a chance to find out where he was he shut them again with a groan. Never in his life had he had such a headache. The whole area beneath his skull was a searing, jolting mass of pain.

After a moment he opened his eyes once more. He was lying on a narrow, old-fashioned steel bed from whose frame the paint had flaked badly. Beside him, on another bed, lay Stephen; still unconscious but beginning to stir. Across the room, as his eyes focused in the sunlight, he could see Kenny, still spark out. Of Carol there was no sign.

He looked around. The three of them were lying in what looked like a small hospital ward. At the door two military policeman stood, broad-shouldered and stony-faced. One of them, seeing John stir, did a smart about-turn and disappeared. In a moment a doctor appeared, dressed in army uniform beneath his white coat.

He treated John to a small, professional smile, making him feel that it was a luxury to which he was not entitled.

'How do you feel?' he asked, testing his pulse.

'My head . . . it aches terribly,' John told him.

'Hmm. I wonder why,' said the doctor. Without another word, he turned on his heel and went away.

A few moments later a nurse appeared with tablets and a glass of water. She was pretty but her expression was that of a stone statue.

'What are these?' John asked, looking at the tablets suspiciously.

Drugs, as well as alcohol and cigarettes, anything that could impair the efficiency of their minds, the Tomorrow People avoided like poison.

'Just aspirins,' said the nurse.

John swallowed them with a sip of water. The nurse, like the doctor before her, gave him the tiniest of smiles.

'It looks as though your friends are ready for some, too,' she said.

John could see that Stephen and Kenny had now recovered consciousness.

As his head cleared a succession of wild questions formed themselves in John's mind.

That the army had captured them was only too clear. But how had it happened? What had made them lose consciousness? Did their captors know that they had come there to make contact with the visitor from outer space?

John sighed as he passed a hand across his forehead. Somewhere in that same building was the creature they had come to rescue. For the moment, though, there was no point in worrying about his problems. They had sufficient of their own.

Looking at the bed beside him, he could see that Stephen was fully conscious. The nurse was bending over him.

'What happened, Stephen?' he asked – though he didn't expect Stephen to remember any more than he did.

'No talking!'

It was one of the military policemen who barked from his post by the door.

Looking across at the coarse, arrogant face under the peaked cap, John suddenly felt a wave of anger; a desire to teach the man a sharp lesson. Instinctively, he felt for the stun gun which he normally carried at his waist. It was not there. Only then did he realize that his clothes had been taken away and that he had been dressed in rough military pyjamas several sizes too large for him.

He relaxed with a sigh, feeling suddenly ashamed of himself. Of course, he had been wrong to want to paralyse the man merely because he had been offensive. Their gifts were not to be spent on acts of petty spite. That kind of thing was for Saps.

The military policeman's curt order had not intimidated Stephen. Turning to look at John, he sent:

'We tried to make contact with the visitor. It looks as though this is the result.'

The military policeman knew nothing about telepathy. As long as there was no talking he was happy. Across the ward the nurse had brought more aspirins for Kenny, who was now coming round.

As his head cleared, everything came back to John in stark detail. Carol, he remembered, had warned him that it might be dangerous to send to the visitor – and she had been right. He wished that he had followed her advice and contacted TIM first. But it was too late to worry about that now.

The army doctor reappeared, his professional smile engraved on his face.

'Feeling better now?' he asked.

'Yes thank you,' John replied.

'Good,' said the doctor. 'Then you're ready for Colonel M. He's got a lot of questions to ask you.'

The doctor turned on his heel and went away but the four did not have long to wait. Five minutes later, another military policeman, a sergeant, appeared carrying their clothes over his arm. He threw the three boys the garments which had been taken from them when they were captured.

'Right,' he said. 'Get dressed.'

'What about my . . .' said John. He had been going to ask about his jaunting-belt, his communicator and his stun gun. But he stopped, realizing that it would be useless.

'No questions,' said the sergeant. 'Just get dressed.'

John, looking at him, realized that he was older than his two comrades. There was something frank and decent in his face, but John searched in vain for any trace of expression.

When they had dressed, the man looked them up and down, for all the world as though he were looking for an unpolished shoe or a dirty button.

'Ready?' he said.

They nodded.

'Good,' said the sergeant. 'Follow me.'

The two guards fell into step behind them and the procession made its way down a dark, narrow corridor to a door which faced them at the end.

'Halt here,' said the sergeant. It was not a parade-ground bark; he spoke quite gently.

They waited while he knocked briskly at the door.

'Come!'

Even through the thickness of the door the voice inside sounded unmistakably stern and military.

The sergeant stepped into the room and snapped to attention.

'The other three have recovered now, sir,' he said.

'Good. Bring them in,' the voice ordered.

The sergeant stepped aside and motioned them to enter. The guards took up their rigid positions outside the door.

Like everything else they had seen in the centre the room was bleak and sparsely-furnished. There was not a touch of colour anywhere to relieve the drab, watery green of the walls, or the grubby white of the ceiling.

Carol was sitting to one side of the room, a military policewoman behind her. She smiled at them wanly.

At a desk before the window sat two officers. John recognized them instantly as the men whom he had seen speaking to the police superintendent on the shore at Kilgardie.

One was a colonel: aged about fifty, he had broad shoulders and a short, thick neck. His iron-grey hair was slicked down smartly and his clipped, toothbrush moustache was also flecked with grey. This, presumably, was Colonel M – the name used by the local head of military intelligence.

The man beside him was a captain in his mid-thirties. Slim and fair-haired, he was plainly trying to appear as severe and forbidding as the colonel, but not quite bringing it off.

On the desk before them lay the Tomorrow People's equipment: jaunting-belts, stun guns, memory erasers and communicators. Momentarily, John wondered what had happened to the electro-scanners. Perhaps they were being examined in another part of the building.

The colonel looked at them keenly for a moment, his expression relaxing a fraction as he noticed their pallor. Though their heads were rapidly clearing, none of them yet felt really well.

'You'd better sit down,' said the colonel. His voice, like his moustache, was clipped. 'Chairs, sergeant, please.'

Swiftly the sergeant slid three chairs from their place beside the wall.

When they had seated themselves, Colonel M spoke again.

'You know where you are?' he asked, curtly.

'Yes sir,' said John. 'We are in the medical research centre on the shore of Loch Derrig.'

'Right,' said the colonel. 'Now perhaps you will tell me what you are doing here. In particular, how you came to be lying unconscious beside the perimeter fence.'

'We were camping,' John told him, innocently. 'At least, we were going to.'

'Camping? Out here?' The colonel's voice was hard, disbelieving.

'We were told it was very pretty here,' put in Carol, helpfully.

Colonel M turned his steel-blue eyes towards her.

'Were you not also told that this is a maximum-security military establishment,' he demanded. 'That the entire loch is strictly barred to all visitors?'

'No, I'm sorry, we weren't,' Carol replied. Her expression of demure contrition would have melted a lesser man than Colonel M.

The captain spoke for the first time.

'How did you get here?' he asked.

They all searched their imaginations frantically for a plausible reply.

'We, er . . . hiked,' said Stephen, after a moment.

'Hiked? Over the mountains? In the dark?'

The two officers stared at them, waiting again for a reply. When none was forthcoming, the colonel spoke again.

'We know you have come from Kilgardie,' he said. 'You were seen there – we saw you ourselves. You pitched your tents there, in a field owned by a crofter named McCaig. The tents are still there at this moment.'

So, they had been watched; their every movement checked. John wondered whether they had been suspected from the beginning.

'Now,' said the colonel, changing tack abruptly. 'Let's see if you can answer the other part of my question – truthfully, this time. Who, or what, knocked you unconscious?'

Again they strove for some kind of explanation which Colonel M might just possibly believe. Again it was Stephen who made a brave try – following up a telepathed suggestion from John.

'It must have been those lights you switched on so suddenly, when it was so dark. That and the helicopter engine. It was so loud! Noise can knock you out, sir, so I've been told.'

The colonel smiled, a hard little smile.

'It can, laddie,' he said drily. 'But it takes more than a few landing lights and a helicopter engine to knock four healthy youngsters out all at once. So you'll have to do better than that.'

There was a moment's silence. Colonel M twirled a gold pencil between his fingers, studying it as though it might tell him something important. Finally, he laid it down on his blotting-pad and motioned with his hand at their equipment, lying on the desk before him.

'What's all this stuff?' he demanded, abruptly.

'Oh, it's just camping-gear,' said John, vaguely.

The colonel's eyebrows shot up.

'And things we use for playing games in the woods,' added John, desperately. There was no escape from their predicament. They *could* jaunt, of course; but they could not travel far without belts, otherwise they were likely to go badly off course. And in any case, at this stage they did not want to risk giving themselves away.

It was essential, if possible, to convince their interrogator that they were indeed four ordinary youngsters.

Colonel M picked up a stun gun in one hand and a memory-eraser in the other.

'This stuff never came from any toy-shop,' he said, 'It's scientific equipment of some kind. Now, what is it? What is it used for?'

None of them answered him. They could think of nothing to say. John wondered what the colonel was making of them: how much he had guessed about their real purpose in coming to this remote part of Scotland. Did he suspect, however dimly, that they might be Tomorrow People? If so, the outlook was bleak indeed.

Colonel M sighed and leaned back. He replaced the pistol and the memory eraser on the desk.

'Well, we're not getting very far, are we?'

John thought that, just for a second, he detected a tired, strained edge to the clipped, meticulous voice. It was as though he was seriously worried but did not want to show it.

'You'd be wiser to answer our questions. Help us to help you, you know.'

It was the captain who spoke now, anxious to have his five pennyworth. For the first time Carol noticed that he had a rather weak chin.

The colonel leaned forward again, his eyes boring keenly into John's face. His shoulders tensed and the knuckles of his clasped hands showed white. John was sure that he was about to start shouting, but when he spoke his voice was still quiet. It was plain that he was making a big effort to master his anger.

'Now look,' he said. 'You might as well come clean,

because we know a great deal more than you think we do.'

The four Tomorrow People braced themselves, fearful of what might be coming.

'Yes,' continued Colonel M, his voice full of quiet menace. 'We know you are not of our kind . . .'

They caught their breath. Was it really possible that he knew their secret? Or was this some wild bluff – a mere guess which had come perilously near to the mark?

'. . . and we know what you were after when you landed outside there. We've got your friend and we're sticking to him until you tell us all that we want to know.'

Once again it was John who spoke. He was growing more and more puzzled. What did Colonel M mean when he said they were 'not of our kind'?

'We were not trespassing when you found us – at least, we were outside the camp perimeter. You have no right to keep us here.'

'No – and you have no right to ask these questions, either,' put in Carol.

Colonel M grinned nastily.

'I haven't, eh?' he said. 'And what about all this stuff?'

Once again he motioned towards the equipment on the desk. 'Not so easy to explain that away, is it?'

He leaned forward again. 'And what's more,' he declared triumphantly, 'we know that you are no use without it. While we have got it, there's absolutely nothing you can do to help yourselves. So if you ever want to see your home again – wherever it is -- you had better talk!'

All four of them remained silent, waiting for the colonel's rage to break over them at last. Still he kept himself in check. It was almost as though he were a little – just a little – afraid.

Eventually, he stood up.

'Right,' he said crisply. 'I don't propose to waste any more time now. You can have a couple of hours to think over your position, and by that time I hope that you'll have decided to be sensible.'

He nodded to the sergeant who opened the door behind them. They filed out and were marched back down the corridor, past the ward which the boys had occupied, to another room at the far end.

'In here,' said the sergeant, opening the door.

This room, too, was bleak in the extreme. They all noticed at once that the windows were high and barred. A table and four chairs formed the only furniture.

'You feeling hungry?' the sergeant asked, as they settled themselves.

They suddenly realized that they were extremely hungry.

'Right,' said the sergeant. 'I'll see what I can do.'

He turned to go and then paused, as though wondering whether he ought to say what he wanted to say. Finally he stepped back, shutting the door behind him.

'Look,' he said. 'I don't know why you're holding out, but it's going to be best for you if you tell the colonel about yourselves. I mean, it's reasonable, isn't it? You can't expect to come barging down to Earth without somebody wanting to know what it's all about.'

'Barging down to Earth ...?' John began. He was flabbergasted.

'Sure,' said the sergeant. 'The Earth *is* our patch, after all. So at least we've got a right to know which planet you're from.'

CHAPTER SIX

With a hiss and a rumble the underground train moved slowly out of the station, treating its discarded passengers to a low, whining farewell as it disappeared into the tunnel. The assorted throng of theatre-goers and businessmen kept late at the office scurried for the escalators, hardly sparing a glance for the two boys in Hell's Angel jerkins who hung around a chocolate machine at the rear end of the platform.

A West Indian attendant eyed them suspiciously, fearing that they were waiting for a chance to prise it open. But he relaxed when one of them, a ginger-haired lad, put a coin in, extracted his bar of chocolate, and halved it with his mate.

The man turned his back as the two Hell's Angels ambled peaceably up the platform towards him. Probably not real Hell's Angels at all, he told himself. Just wearing the gear so they can look tough.

Watching until the attendant was out of sight, they immediately turned back and raised a small trapdoor hidden close to the tunnel entrance. In a moment they were bent low in a sewer-like gallery which ran off at an angle and eventually brought them to that little-known part of the London Underground which was doomed to remain forever sealed off and silent.

Picking their way deftly along the trackless tunnel which lay before them, they came at last to a solid brick wall which apparently brought the tunnel to an end. Bending, they pushed open a low door and, after another near-crawl through a low gallery, they found themselves at length in the underground laboratory where TIM reigned over the equipment of the Tomorrow People.

'They've disappeared, TIM,' said the red-haired one. 'Their parents are getting worried.'

'Yes Ginge,' replied TIM, 'I am too. I'm glad you have come.'

Ginge and Lefty, both authentic Hell's Angels, were the only Saps in the whole world who knew the secret of the Tomorrow People – apart, of course, from the parents of the four.

Six months previously, they had fallen under the spell of Jedekiah, ostensibly the leader of a new mystic sect, but really an errant robot whom a blown fuse had doomed to wander through the universe causing mischief wherever he could. In dealing with Jedekiah, the Tomorrow People had eventually made Ginge and Lefty see that they were in the grip of an evil force, and had taken them into their confidence. Now TIM had work for them.

The computer had received no word from the four for more than twelve hours. Clearly, therefore, they had fallen into the hands of the military at Loch Derrig and their equipment had been taken from them. Somehow. it had to be replaced: TIM had to get new jaunting-belts to them, and new stun guns. Otherwise, they had little chance of escape.

And so it was that two Hell's Angels rode into the valley of Loch Derrig, carrying an array of gadgets that would have made them the envy of any motorway chapter in the kingdom.

As the flat-roofed buildings came into sight Ginge waved his friend to a halt. Carefully, they dismounted and pressed themselves into the bracken at the side of the road.

'Well one thing's for sure, Lefty,' said Ginge. 'They don't believe in giving you a Highland welcome.' He waved at the barbed wire which surrounded the centre.

Lefty nodded vigorously.

'So,' continued Ginge, 'it looks as though we gotta use a bit of the old subterfuge.'

Lefty nodded once more.

'Right then. You fall off – I'll do the talking.'

They climbed back on to their machines. With a kick and a roar they moved off along the road which ran beside the loch, towards the clump of buildings where they knew the Tomorrow People were held prisoner.

As the barbed wire of the centre loomed larger Ginge could see men in uniform watching them through fieldglasses. If all that TIM had told them was true, he thought, the soldiers must be pretty jumpy. Let's hope they don't rumble us.

He slowed a little to let Lefty pass him, praying that Lefty would not put too much into his performance. If his friend succeeded in laying himself out, or even injured himself seriously . . . well, it just didn't bear thinking of. They'd got problems enough already.

He need not have worried. Accelerating away, Lefty suddenly wobbled, spun from one side of the road to the other, and finished up face downwards in the bracken. His machine careered, riderless, across the road to stop, wheels spinning, in the reeds. It was a beautiful performance, one that any film stunt man would have been proud of.

As Ginge braked to a halt and ran to his friend, conscious that keen eyes were watching, he wondered for a moment whether Lefty had overdone it. But a swift wink told him that all was well.

As he knelt beside Lefty's recumbent form, a Land-Rover screamed out of the gate in front of him and covered the two hundred yards' distance in a few seconds. In it were two men – the captain who had helped Colonel M in his interrogation, and a young military police corporal.

'What the hell's going on here?' barked the captain, jumping down from the Land-Rover.

'He's fallen off,' Ginge wailed.

'I can see that he's fallen off, you fool,' the officer snapped. He knelt down beside Lefty and turned him over.

'You better hadn't touch him, mister – he might have broken something,' warned Ginge.

'Shut up,' ordered the captain. Jumping to his feet, he turned to the corporal.

'Better get Major Dobson,' he said.

'Very good, sir,' said the corporal. Springing into the Land-Rover, he raced back towards the medical centre.

'Confounded young idiots,' stormed the captain, turning back to Ginge. 'You're not fit to be on the road. What do you think you're doing round here anyway?'

'Just riding,' said Ginge.

For the first time the captain became aware of his accent. He stared at Ginge, suspiciously.

'You're from London, aren't you?' he asked.

'Yeah, that's right, guv'nor,' said Ginge. 'Just come to get away from the smoke, you know.'

'Well why, with the entire blasted Highlands to choose from, do you have to pick this spot to land yourselves in a mess?'

Ginge had been right. The officer was distinctly edgy. Glancing at the centre Ginge wondered which building the Tomorrow People were in.

'It just happened,' he told the captain plaintively. 'I mean, he just skidded. It could have happened to anyone.'

'You've no right to be in the valley at all,' retorted the captain. 'There are notices warning visitors to stay away.'

'We must have missed them,' Ginge told him. He tried to look suitably contrite.

The captain turned impatiently, looking towards the centre to see whether his colleague was coming.

'You will help him, won't you?' said Ginge. 'You

51

will take him in? I know you got doctors in there. There aren't any hospitals for miles.'

The captain turned back sharply.

'Who told you we've got doctors?' he demanded.

'It's a medical centre, isn't it?' asked Ginge. 'Stands to reason you have.'

The captain eyed him for a moment before replying.

'Major Dobson's a doctor,' he said. 'He will decide what's necessary.'

At last the Land-Rover roared up once more and Major Dobson alighted. He was the same doctor who had treated the Tomorrow People.

Deftly he raised Lefty's eyelid and frowned.

'Not much sign of concussion,' he murmured. 'Still . . .'

He turned to the captain.

'Better get him inside,' he said. 'I'll take a proper look at him there. If necessary, we'll get an ambulance from Kintooloch.'

Under Major Dobson's supervision, Ginge and the corporal loaded the silent form into the back seat of the Land-Rover. With the air of a man whose patience was almost at breaking-point, the captain turned to Ginge.

'I suppose you'd better come as well,' he said. 'Corporal Lewis will help you with the other bike.'

Muttering to the major, he climbed behind the wheel as the major joined him in the front. The Land-Rover shot away once more.

'Don't mind him,' said Corporal Lewis, a cheery young man. 'Things have been a bit fraught here these past twenty-four hours.'

Soon they were inside the camp. Ginge, straining his eyes for a glimpse of his friends, could still see no sign of them – or of the space-visitor.

Lefty had been placed in the ward where John, Stephen and Kenny had lain a short time before. When Ginge and the corporal entered, he was lying fully-dressed on one of the beds, still apparently unconscious.

The major was looking down at him; a trifle suspiciously, Ginge thought.

'I must say, I thought he'd have come round by now,' muttered the major. He pondered for a moment.

'Better take his jerkin off – and his boots,' he said.

At once Lefty's eyes fluttered and he groaned – a superbly convincing groan. But it was too late. Already the corporal had moved forward and unzipped the jerkin. Round Lefty's waist, clearly exposed, were the two jaunting-belts which he had fastened there before leaving the lab.

The captain stood transfixed, his eyes starting from his head. He pointed at Ginge.

'Quick,' he yelled. 'Grab him!'

With a bound, Ginge jumped back towards the door, yanking a stun gun from each pocket of his jerkin. Three quick bursts and each of the men was frozen immobile.

'Come on, Lefty,' he muttered breathlessly. 'We haven't got any time to lose.'

In a flash, Lefty was on his feet. Pistols at the ready, they raced out into the corridor, turned a corner and found two sentries guarding the door of a room at the end.

Seeing the two Hell's Angels, the men were taken aback for a split second. Then they reached for their revolvers.

Once again, Ginge beat them to it. A couple of quick bursts and they, too, stood as stiff as statues.

'Right,' said Ginge. 'In here.'

The four Tomorrow People were sitting round the bare table. They looked up expecting one of their captors to enter and the expression on their faces when they recognized their two friends would have made Ginge howl with laughter if only he'd had the time.

Swiftly, the two Hell's Angels produced the jaunting-belts from their waists.

'Right,' said Ginge. 'You jaunt. We'll shoot our way out.'

'Can't do that,' replied John.

'What do you mean,' cried Ginge in alarm.

'The visitor's still in here somewhere,' said Stephen. 'We can't leave without him.'

'Are you crazy?' demanded Ginge. But he knew that to argue would be a waste of time. When the Tomorrow People had a job to do they did it, no matter how great the danger.

Cautiously, they opened the door and crept out into the corridor, past the two immobile sentries. In half an hour they would come out of their trance, along with the officers. They would not know how much time had passed, and there would be a frantic search for the Tomorrow People. By that time, they would have to be clean away – and the visitor with them.

The building was one of the single-storey blocks lying close to the main gate. Carol remembered that when the visitor had been flown in, he had been taken at first to the upper storey of the taller building. Was he still there? They couldn't be sure, but it seemed as likely a place as any.

Eyes darting everywhere, they stole across a wide concrete path to the door of the building on which the helicopter had touched down. As they reached it, a white-coated orderly marched smartly out.

'What the . . .?' he demanded, but got no further. Lefty froze him with a squirt. Ginge grinned delightedly.

'He doesn't say much, my mate, but he knows when to do the needful,' he observed.

Slowly, they moved along another narrow corridor towards a flight of stairs. Not a soul was in sight.

'I don't think much of their security,' muttered Stephen.

'They're not used to anyone getting past the main gate,' John told him. 'And apart from that, I don't think they ever expected to get a visit from outer space.'

The rooms of the ground floor were all laboratories. A glance at the complicated equipment would have told a Sap nothing, unless he happened to be a trained bacteriologist. To the Tomorrow People, however, its use was plain; the research centre was primarily concerned with germ warfare. John was right; none of the staff was especially equipped to cope with a being from a remote planet.

Cautiously, they turned the corner where the stairs ran upwards, at right angles from the corridor. At once they saw the now-familiar sight of a pair of sentries wearing the red caps of the military police. They goggled at the six youngsters, then reached for their revolvers.

'No you don't,' yelled John, pointing his stun gun at them. It was a piece of bluff, for he knew that the pistol would not freeze anyone at that range. The bluff worked. The men hesitated just long enough for John to bound up the stairs towards them. As they brought their revolvers out, he reached the top of the stairs and gave each of them a swift squirt. They remained rigid, their hands on their holsters.

As the others ran up the stairs behind him, John flung open the door. The room was exactly like the one in which he and his three companions had been detained. Inside were four people; three of whom jumped to their feet at once.

Two of these were doctors, white coats over their uniforms. The third was Colonel M.

'Right – back against the wall!' ordered John.

The doctors obeyed swiftly, their hands raised. Colonel M remained where he was, eyeing John's pistol as though trying to make up his mind whether it was real.

Kenny pushed past John, waving his pistol menacingly.

'Go on, colonel. Move!' he piped. Slowly, the colonel joined his two colleagues, who were now standing against the wall.

While Kenny covered the three of them, the others turned their attention to the fourth occupant of the room. He had remained motionless at the table, watching everything with silent interest.

As they looked at him their jaws dropped.

'Cor,' said Ginge. 'It's a kid!'

He was right. The visitor from outer space was a child. At the most, he could be no more than six years old.

He sat there looking back at them, a puzzled, pleased smile playing about his lips. It was obvious that he didn't quite realize what was happening, but he grasped that somehow the tables had been turned.

For a moment they looked at one another in silence. Then Carol stepped across to the table, smiling down at the little boy. After a moment's hesitation, the child smiled back – a huge, delighted grin.

As she looked down at him, Carol thought that she had never seen anyone so attractive. He was dressed in a mauve, one-piece suit, made of some translucent material never seen on Earth, which glowed and shimmered gently in the afternoon sunlight. His complexion might have been called sallow, save that it had a beautiful egg shell consistency which no advertisement for cosmetics could ever hope to equal. His eyes, glowing under a mop of dark curls, were a remarkable shade of purple. His head and ears tapered to the finest of points.

Carol was about to telepath a greeting when John laid a hand on her arm.

'Remember what happened last time,' he said.

Each of the Tomorrow People threw up a telepathic screen – the equivalent of pressing their hands over their ears – before Carol proceeded to communicate with the little boy.

'We are friends,' she telepathed. 'We have come to help you.'

Despite the precaution which they had taken, the

response almost blasted them off their feet. They had no doubt now that it was the space-child who had unwittingly knocked them unconscious.

'Here, steady on!' cried Ginge. He stepped forward to catch Kenny, who had almost fallen over.

Colonel M, seeing a chance, stepped forward and reached for his revolver.

'No you don't!' yelled Ginge.

But it was Lefty who waved his stun gun menacingly. The colonel stepped back, biting his lip in anger.

Carol telepathed to the child once more.

'Try to speak quietly,' she told him. 'Whisper.'

The child nodded vigorously.

'Now,' Carol telepathed. 'Where are you from?'

The little boy shook his head. No longer smiling, he appeared on the verge of tears. Carol was reminded of a toddler she had once seen lost in a department store, too young to tell the worried assistants where he lived.

'Don't worry,' thought Carol. 'We'll get you out of here, then we'll see about getting you home again.'

The child sniffed, attempting a brave smile.

Kenny stepped forward. The little visitor stared at him, obviously intrigued by his dark skin.

'What's your name?' Kenny asked him.

For the first time they got an answer that was loud and clear, without battering at their brains. It consisted of a single word:

'Arlon.'

It was John who now took over again.

'Right, Arlon,' he said. 'First of all, we've got to get out of here.'

The child nodded even more vigorously than before.

Pointing at the three officers against the wall, he declared,

'Bad men.'

John glanced at them, then turned back to the child.

'Not bad,' he replied. 'Just stupid.'

'Who's stupid?'

To their astonishment, the colonel's clipped voice had interrupted their conversation.

'Who's stupid?' he repeated.

It was then that they realized, with a shock, that Colonel M was himself telepathic – though apparently only slightly so. He had picked up John's remark. They knew, of course, that some Saps had limited telepathic powers; the colonel apparently was one of them. In future, they would have to be extremely careful.

Recovering quickly, Stephen gave him a condescending smile.

'On our planet,' he explained, 'we converse by telepathic means all the time. It's our normal mode of speech.'

Ginge's brow furrowed. Sometimes, like all Saps, he could be a little slow on the uptake.

'On your planet?' he asked. 'What d'you mean . . .'

Before he could get any further, Carol gave him a swift kick. Ginge's mouth snapped shut.

The colonel, a crafty interrogator, had avoided telling the Tomorrow People what conclusions he had formed about them, but the military police sergeant had given the game away. If the military thought that the four of them, like Arlon, came from another planet, that suited the Tomorrow People very well indeed. Let them go on thinking so. Their secret – their real secret – remained safe, and that was of over-riding importance.

Clearly, Colonel M and his colleagues must believe that they had somehow taken over the identities of four ordinary youngsters. John wondered what they had made of Ginge and Lefty. Did they think that the two Hell's Angels had also come from a distant planet?

There was no time to find out. Soon the first of the victims – the men who had brought Ginge and Lefty into the centre – would be recovering from the effects of the stun gun. They had to get away before that happened, for they could no longer rely on the element of surprise.

John leaned forward and sent carefully to the little figure before him.

'Can you jaunt?' he asked.

The child looked puzzled. John paused, then formed a mental picture of a little boy jaunting over a short distance. Arlon shook his head.

The Tomorrow People looked at one another.

'He doesn't even know what jaunting means,' said Kenny.

While Stephen and John covered the three Sap officers, Carol took Arlon's hand and led him, past the two transfixed guards, out into the sunshine. Kenny went too, along with Ginge and Lefty, but he paused to take a bunch of keys from the pocket of one of the guards.

He brought them back to John.

'That's the one you need,' he said, showing him the one that fitted the door.

'Thanks,' said John, as Kenny went to join the others. Then he spoke to the prisoners.

'Turn and face the wall, and don't try to come after us – at least, not until we're well away,' he warned. 'You may feel stupid being locked in here, but you'll feel even more stupid if we paralyse you.'

'You'll never get away . . .' Colonel M blustered, as the three men obeyed John's command.

But John and Stephen didn't wait to hear more. Slamming the door, they locked it behind them and raced out into the concrete yard in front of the main building. There the four Tomorrow People joined hands to form a link with Carol and Kenny holding fast to Arlon.

'Let's hope this works,' murmured John. 'Hold him tight.'

They jaunted. Lefty and Ginge, watching from their bikes saw the four Tomorrow People disappear effortlessly. Little Arlon was left alone in the middle of the wide expanse of concrete.

'They've left the kid!' shouted Ginge and started forward. Even as Ginge ran towards him, Arlon, with a startled look on his face, slowly dematerialized.

Carol and Kenny felt they were being torn apart. It was like trying to pull an elephant out of quicksand. The fleeting rainbow confusion of hyperspace tumbled all around them. Through them also flowed the linked power of John and Stephen. Pulling, forcing, squeezing little Arlon through the vortex.

They were trembling when they arrived in the Lab, all four of them. They stared in horrified fascination at the empty space between them where Arlon ought to be.

Kenny could feel him, holding on tight. The waves of grim terror flooding out of the little alien boy, wherever or whenever he was, threatened to make them all lose consciousness.

A misty shadow came and went. They used their linked minds to concentrate with a desperate intensity. TIM extended his link contacts towards them. John and Stephen risked breaking the circle to grab at the contacts. In that microsecond they almost lost Arlon for ever. Then with the tremendous added power of TIM they managed to pull him through. The whole Lab shook with energy as the little shadow became an outline, the outline became a shape and the shape slowly solidified. Suddenly there was Arlon, standing between them in the Lab with a very puzzled look on his face.

'Phew!' breathed John collapsing into a chair. 'I don't want to go through that again.'

Lefty and Ginge stared at the spot where Arlon had vanished.

'I hope he's got through all right,' said Ginge. Then they kicked their bikes into life and roared out of the Centre to begin the dangerous but enjoyable task of dodging the road blocks on the long ride back to London.

CHAPTER SEVEN

The citizens of Kilgardie, after a day of anxious speculation, came to the conclusion that the strange object now lying submerged so close to their shore must be a highly-secret guided missile which had somehow wandered from its testing-range.

The over-thirties, remembering the war-time posters which warned that 'Careless Talk Costs Lives', decided that the less said about it the better. Who could tell, some enterprising agent from Eastern Europe may already have heard that the object which had shot across the sky on the previous evening was to be found just below the waves which washed against their village. If such a one should appear, no matter how clever his disguise, he would hear nothing to his advantage from the dour patriots of Kilgardie.

The villagers were encouraged in this reticence by

Colonel M and his trusty captain, who let it be known, via the local police, that any indiscretion might well constitute a breach of the Official Secrets Act, with all the dire consequences which that entailed.

The two officers then paid a visit to the McCaigs, where they collected the Tomorrow People's camping gear for examination and gleaned what information they could. This turned out to be very little. The four had been well-mannered youngsters who, though a trifle quiet, had given no reason to doubt their complete ordinariness.

Colonel M and the captain went on their way, counselling the McCaigs to say nothing about their visit to the neighbours and to avoid all questions about the youngsters' sudden disappearance. This emphasis on secrecy sprang partly from a desire not to alarm the public at large, and partly from a desire not to broadcast the fact that three boys and a girl had succeeded in making fools of military intelligence. Somehow, the thought that they were almost certainly from some superior civilization on another planet did little to take the sting away.

Meanwhile, in the underground laboratory, the Tomorrow People had all but given up their vain attempt to teach Arlon the basic principles of jaunting.

'It's useless,' declared John, mopping his forehead in exhaustion. 'It's a complete waste of time. He simply can't grasp it.'

TIM, clicking and whirring gently, refrained from saying: 'I told you so.' By dint of much patient questioning, they had got the boy to tell them everything that he possibly could about his home planet. Since he was a bright little chap, even by the standards of the Tomorrow People, this amounted to quite a lot. When they fed it all to TIM, he had swiftly assured them that not only did Arlon's compatriots not know how to jaunt, but they were completely incapable of being taught.

'Perhaps,' TIM had concluded, 'that is why their space-ship technology is so highly developed. They have been forced by their own limitations to invent some other highly efficient means of superluminary travel.'

Despite TIM's findings and their experiences on the return from Kilgardie, John had resolved to try whether Arlon couldn't just possibly be taught to jaunt, even if only for very short distances. Some day, he argued, a people so advanced in other ways must acquire the ability to travel through hyperspace. Perhaps Arlon would turn out to be one of the first, just as they themselves had been the first on Earth . . .

It was a hope born of desperation. If Arlon couldn't jaunt then it looked as though he were likely to be a prisoner in the underground lab until they could send him back in his space-ship.

The Tomorrow People knew that it would not be long before the Saps recovered the ship and the prospect was an extremely worrying one. Sap scientists had made enormous strides in space technology during the past ten years and they were capable of learning a great deal from Arlon's vehicle.

If the Saps succeeded in constructing one half as efficient, they would spread out across the universe in no time, with possible consequences that did not bear thinking of. Saps simply were not civilized enough to make contact with people on other planets. They would go in friendship, bearing gifts; but all too soon they would want to conquer and destroy. One did not have to be a Tomorrow Person to realize that: the lesson was there in the history books for anyone to read.

Arlon, as they suspected, came from a planet far out in deep space; he couldn't tell them where, but from his description, it sounded as though it was well beyond Andromeda.

When they asked him what it was called, Arlon screwed up his eyes and made a big effort to remember, trying at the same time not to burst into tears. Eventually, he looked at them with a mixture of hope and doubt. 'I think it's called Crito,' he said.

More questions revealed that the Critons were a wise, peaceful people who were well advanced in many branches of technology, but above all in space travel. They had long ago banished war from their own civilization, but some of their nearer neighbours had not yet reached this stage of development and were prone to invade Crito in the hope of taking over so attractive a planet.

The Critons, therefore, were obliged to maintain a strong defensive system whose main element was a space-fleet of ten thousand ships. These patrolled constantly at a distance of twenty light-years from the planet's surface. Arlon's father, Saav, was a captain in this fleet. He was in charge of a squadron of twenty ships.

One day, Arlon persuaded Saav to take him up on patrol – a request which turned out to have disastrous consequences. Attached to each squadron was a life-ship, an empty, computer-driven vehicle which was for use only in an emergency. If a regular ship was damaged or suffered mechanical failure, the life-ship could be used to carry the crew safely back to the planet's surface; or, if they were too far from home, to the surface of the nearest planet which would support life.

While his father's back was turned, Arlon had wandered to the far end of the command ship and had begun to fiddle about with the escape-mechanism. Suddenly, he had been ejected into space. The command-ship, with his unsuspecting father still busy at the controls, shot rapidly away from him.

For a moment, Arlon drifted helplessly in his space-suit, crying out for help even though he knew that no one could hear. Then the life-ship, as it was pro-grammed to do, sucked him towards it magnetically and opened its entrance-hatch to allow him inside.

An older and more sensible child would then have sat quietly and allowed the life-ship to carry him back to Crito. But Arlon, by now thoroughly terrified, simply panicked.

Making a grab at the manual controls, he tried to steer the life-ship towards his father's craft so that his father would see him and come to his aid. As soon as he touched the controls, the computer shut down and the ship began to career through space at superluminary speed, in the opposite direction to Crito and safety.

By this time, the entire space-fleet had been alerted and half-a-dozen squads raced after the life-ship in a vain effort to catch it. In his terror, however, Arlon had pressed down on the speed-button and the ships, although they kept on his tail for more than fifty thousand light-years, were unable to catch him.

Frantically, Saav shouted instructions over the radio to his now-petrified little boy: told him again and again which buttons he must press to slow the life-ship and allow the computer to take over.

When Arlon eventually understood and did what was necessary, it was too late. The space-fleet had lost track of the ship among the stars of Andromeda. Already well beyond their normal range, they could only turn back sadly for home, Saav beside himself with grief.

In the life-ship, Arlon lost consciousness as the computer took over again and steered the craft onwards through space. Its superluminary drive was beginning to weaken when it finally entered our solar system, but the computer was still functioning strongly and at once it registered the life-bearing properties of Earth.

Unerringly, it homed in on the unknown planet, ejecting Arlon to safety as soon as it had settled itself on the soft bed of the sea. The little boy had floated ashore on the midnight tide in a space-suit which had been given a special buoyancy by its designers precisely so that it would support the occupant if he had to land in water.

Even though TIM had forewarned them, the Tomorrow People had not realized until now just what an enormous setback they had to face. It had seemed incredible that a youngster from a civilization so highly developed would turn out to be completely incapable of jaunting.

While the four of them sat down to discuss the next

move, Arlon sat on a high stool, sucking a lollipop which Kenny had found in his pocket, and blinking curiously at TIM.

'When we brought him back from Kilgardie,' mused Carol, 'he wasn't wearing a belt but we still got him through.'

'Only just,' said Kenny.

'What I'm driving at,' Carol continued, 'is that we ought to try him jaunting with a belt on. We haven't tried it yet.'

Stephen seemed to think it was worth a trial. 'It's the only thing we haven't attempted and with the belt on we could tap TIM's power.'

'We know the belts don't cause us to jaunt. They merely amplify our jaunting power and help us to navigate and materialize again in the right place and not in outer space or deep inside the Earth's crust,' said John. 'We'd be taking quite a risk.'

'But the belt might initiate a jaunt with Arlon and if it did it would navigate him correctly wouldn't it?' Carol argued. 'I don't see we could lose anything by trying.'

'Something could very easily be lost.' It was TIM who had interjected. All turned towards him.

'Arlon could be lost,' said TIM gravely. 'I had to practically drain the National Grid to get enough power to pull him through last time. I couldn't guarantee that on a long-distance jaunt little Arlon wouldn't get lost altogether.'

'You mean lost in hyperspace, TIM?' asked Stephen.

'Exactly,' said TIM. 'We simply don't know enough about his molecular biology to be able to forecast what would happen if you attempted to jaunt him in the teleporter. You might arrive safely, but he might never rematerialize. And if that happened, there'd be no going back for him. Almost certainly, he'd be stranded for ever.'

Each of them shuddered inwardly at TIM's words. They knew little about the strange other-universe of hyperspace, save that it was dark and that many of the laws of nature which operated in our space were suspended or even reversed. The life-forms which existed there were grotesque and horrible. To whirl around there endlessly, without hope of release, was a danger to which they dare not expose little Arlon.

'Somehow, we've got to get hold of that life-ship,' said John, his forehead creased with worry.

'I know,' said Carol. 'But how?'

'Half the Navy will be poking about off Kilgardie by now,' put in Stephen. 'It's only a matter of time before they find it.'

They sat for a moment in silence, wondering how they could best tackle the enormous problem that faced them. Arlon, meanwhile, had moved on to examine the jaunting-belts which were stored on the other side of the lab. Still sucking his lollipop, he was placidly unaware of the obstacles which now lay between him and his faraway home.

Once more, TIM's quiet voice broke in on their thoughts.

'It looks as though there has been a development,' he said.

By means of the observer satellite, TIM had been keeping a careful watch on the search for the life-ship.

He now flashed on to his video-screen the scene at the spot where the ship had finally hovered and disappeared below the waves.

As Stephen had guessed, there was now an enormous number of craft circling round the area: dozens of patrol-boats, a couple of destroyers and six large salvage ships, their lifting-gear prominently displayed.

Clearly, something significant had just happened. From all sides, boats were racing up to a spot marked by one of the destroyers. Then the destroyer moved away and the salvage vessels ranged themselves in two rows, winching down strong cables from the gear on their decks. Grim-faced, the Tomorrow People watched as divers dropped over the ships' sides.

'They've found it,' said John.

He was right. Slowly, the cables were winched in again, the divers surfaced, and soon the long green cylinder of the life-ship rose above the surface of the water.

Unnoticed by the four Tomorrow People, Arlon had crept up to see what they were staring at so intently. His lollipop forgotten, he stood a little behind them, his face puckering as he watched the six salvage vessels steam off to their unknown destination, hauling the smooth, polished surface of the life-ship slowly through the waves.

Although he did not fully comprehend what was happening, Arlon sensed that it boded no good for him. A glance at the expressions of his four friends was more than enough to confirm his apprehension.

Still nobody looked round at him; everyone was utterly intent on the scene on the screen in front of them.

Two big tears rolled down Arlon's cheeks and his face puckered still more. Finally, he let out a long, low howl.

'I want to go home!' he yelled.

CHAPTER EIGHT

When John came round, he found Ginge kneeling
beside him, dabbing at his forehead with a wet cloth.
Next to him, Lefty was doing the same for Kenny. Carol
and Stephen had already recovered consciousness, but
were obviously still very groggy. Carol, pale and heavy-
eyed, was holding on to TIM for support. Stephen was
sitting up on the floor, holding his head in his hands.

As John's brain cleared, he remembered the scene on
the videoscreen. Arlon must have seen it too, and
knocked them all out with the power of his response.
Struggling upright, he looked round for the little
Criton.

'Arlon!' he called. But Arlon was nowhere to be
seen.

John collapsed again with a groan, hit on the head by
what felt like a large steam-hammer.

73

'Steady,' cried Ginge, lowering him again gently.

'Arlon . . . where is he?' asked John.

'He's gone, mate,' replied Ginge. 'He'd vanished when we arrived.'

Since Arlon could not jaunt by himself he could only have escaped through the tunnel which connected the lab to the underground train system. TIM confirmed that this was indeed so. When the Tomorrow People collapsed, the little fellow, overcome with terror, had bolted through the single exit. All TIM's efforts to persuade him to return had been in vain.

'We've got to find him, Ginge,' said John. He attempted to struggle up again, but it was no good. He was still too weak.

'Yes, sure, we'll find him,' said Ginge, soothingly. 'But just take it easy for a few minutes, eh?'

Lefty, silent as always, brought water and aspirins for all four of them. Soon, they began to feel a little better.

'He can't have got far,' said Carol. 'He's probably hiding in the entrance passage.'

Lefty and Ginge looked at one another. Finally, Ginge spoke, his face grave.

'He's not in the passage,' he said. 'He's not anywhere in the approach tunnels. Lefty's already searched.'

Lefty nodded sombrely.

'Then – where is he?' demanded Stephen.

'I don't know,' replied Ginge.

'You mean . . . he's got out?' Carol's expression was now one of horrified disbelief. 'You mean, he's up there somewhere – lost, in the middle of London?'

'Yes,' said Ginge. 'I'm afraid that's about the size of it.'

'Come on,' said John to the others. 'We haven't got any time to lose.'

'Wait a minute.' Ginge laid a hand on his arm. 'There's something you ought to know before you go jaunting off up there.'

'What's that?' John asked.

'They know – all the Saps know – that there's something very peculiar going on. The telly, the papers ... they're full of it.'

'What do you mean?' John demanded.

'Arlon didn't only knock you out,' said Ginge. 'He knocked out fifty thousand young kids as well.'

'What!' All four of them gasped in astonishment.

'That's why we came here,' Ginge continued. 'We knew something had happened to Arlon as soon as we heard the news on TV. Most of those he knocked out were babies and toddlers. It happened right down the country, from the south coast up to Manchester and Leeds, and some in Northern France.'

'You ... you said fifty thousand?' asked Carol.

'They're just the nippers who went out like a light,' said Ginge. 'There were a whole lot more kids – older ones, mostly – who suddenly got splitting headaches, all at the same time. The health authorities are going dotty trying to find out why.'

As the significance of Ginge's news dawned on them clearly, they could hardly contain their excitement.

'So now we know,' said John. 'We've always believed it, but now we know for sure. There are thousands and thousands of us out there.'

'More Tomorrow People waiting to join us,' said Carol, wonderingly. 'Just waiting to break out.'

If there were so many just in one section of England, then how many more were there spread out throughout the world? The number must run into millions.

The day could not be far away when the Tomorrow People would take over from the Saps, and war and strife would finally be banished from the Earth.

However, there was little time to think of that now. Arlon had to be found, quickly.

With swift thanks and farewells, the Tomorrow People left the two Hell's Angels to find their own way to the surface. Then they jaunted, each to a different corner of London, to begin the desperate search for their little friend.

John, landing in Hyde Park, surprised a courting couple who believed that they had the shade of a large elm tree all to themselves. They blinked in astonishment as the lithe youngster appeared from nowhere beside them and strode off across the grass with an anxious frown.

On towards the Serpentine went John, all the time sending out telepathic messages. But never once was there even a flicker of response.

Carol, riding out to North London on the Tube, was meeting with no more success than John. If Arlon had gone in that direction, she wondered, where would he make for? Would Hampstead Heath, with its green, open spaces, attract him? She stopped her reverie, realizing that it was futile. Arlon was a stranger, not only to London, but to Earth itself. He spoke no word of any earthly language. How, then, could he possibly know about Hampstead Heath?

Stephen, who had taken the area south of the river,

jaunted from Brixton to Streatham and from Streatham to Tooting, sending out his telepathic calls with an increasing feeling of hopelessness. Surely, he told himself, if Arlon were somewhere in London, he would have heard and replied by now.

Was it possible that the little boy was receiving their calls perfectly well, and was deliberately refusing to answer? Perhaps he was enjoying himself so much among the new and wonderful sights that he did not choose to return just yet. Perhaps, on the other hand, he had met with some mishap and was lying unconscious and unable to reply. Perhaps he was even . . . but no, Stephen refused to admit that possibility, even to himself. Determination, above all, was what mattered now. If they made up their minds that they were going to find Arlon, find him they would.

Kenny had jaunted out to the East End. He had begun his search in Bethnal Green, the district where he lived, and when that yielded nothing he moved on to Mile End and Whitechapel.

It was here, as he stood outside the Art Gallery, that he got the first faint response to his telepathed calls. It came through so faintly that he was not sure at first whether it was a message from Arlon, or whether it was from some other source – perhaps from a telepathic Sap who happened to be passing. He thought he saw the evening sun shimmering on water and a barge floating stolidly by; then there was nothing.

Standing stock still, straining for every ounce of concentration, he called Arlon again. There was no answer. Once more he tried, still without success. At the third attempt, it came through again – unmistakably the same picture as before. This time he could see it much more clearly, and at once he recognized the scene. It was a spot on the river which he knew well, close to the docks at Poplar. For a moment, it stood out sharp in every detail: the river, the barge, more craft in the background, the sun low in the sky, touching the dark surface of the Thames with gold. Then it broke up and was gone.

Excitedly, Kenny telepathed to the others: 'I think I've found him.'

In a moment, they were by his side. Swiftly, he described what he had seen. Together they jaunted to the spot. They arrived outside the dock gates just in time to see a convoy of police cars come screaming out, with lights flashing and sirens blaring. In the rear of one of them, sandwiched between two large policemen, sat a tiny, frightened figure. It was Arlon.

CHAPTER NINE

Under cover of darkness, and cloaked by the thickest security curtain ever set up in peace-time, the salvage ships and their escort steamed into Holy Loch, where a special berth – a sort of prefabricated hangar on water – had been hastily thrown up to cloak the space-ship from the eyes of the curious.

Within a few hours, the experts arrived; from London, from Washington, from California, from Texas – from every NATO country the defence experts and the scientists came to gaze on the mysterious engine that had brought Arlon from his distant planet at a speed infinitely faster than any of them had dreamed possible.

'Looks kinda simple . . . but I'm durned if I can tell which end is which,' muttered an American general, chomping on his cigar. His colleagues were equally bewildered. None of them had the faintest idea how the space-ship worked.

Colonel M, who had joined the gathering, longed to get his hands once more on the four youngsters who had so recently slipped through his grasp. That they possessed the necessary knowledge, he did not doubt, and he would do everything in his power to make them pass it on.

It was with great joy, therefore, that Colonel M received the news of Arlon's recapture.

The little Criton had found his way to the Tube station above the lab, wandered on to a train and off it again somewhere near the docks. Eventually, he fell asleep behind a pile of packing cases on the wharf, where Kenny managed to locate him. Because he was asleep, he failed to receive the Tomorrow People's calls until it was too late. His drowsy half-response to Kenny had come at the very moment when a keen-eyed young constable spotted him, stirring uneasily on his impromptu bed.

With Arlon back in his power, Colonel M knew that he had only to wait. Before long, the Tomorrow People would be bound to attempt a rescue. This time, he would be ready for them.

After a brief sojourn at Scotland Yard, Arlon was given a sedative and whisked away by helicopter to a country house in Hampshire. To the local people, Tolford Grange was simply a training centre where senior officers came to take advanced courses in a variety of abstruse subjects. In fact, it was a military intelligence centre where many a spy and defector had undergone a gruelling interrogation.

The colonel was confident that the Tomorrow People would never find him there; unless, of course, Arlon managed to signal his whereabouts, and he would have no chance to do that, for the sedative had put him once more into a deep sleep.

When he had satisfied himself that the little boy was comfortable and under the closest possible guard, Colonel M climbed back into the helicopter and set out once more for the research centre by the shores of Loch Derrig. He had a good idea that the Tomorrow People would look for Arlon there.

He showed not a flicker of surprise, therefore, when John and Stephen jaunted into the bleak office and stood before him, stun guns at the ready. Stephen swung swiftly round, expecting to find an armed guard taking aim with his pistol, but apart from the colonel, the room was empty.

'Good morning,' said Colonel M briskly, laying down his pen. 'I was expecting four of you. Where are the others?'

Carol and Kenny had remained behind in the lab, ready to jaunt in as a second wave if John and Stephen needed help. But John did not tell the colonel this. Ignoring the question, he demanded:

'Where's Arlon?'

'He isn't here,' said the colonel.

'We can see that,' said Stephen. 'What have you done with him?'

The colonel regarded them with icy amusement. 'Do put those things away,' he said. 'They won't do you a scrap of good – and they certainly won't help you to find Arlon.'

Slowly, they put away their stun guns and waited for the colonel to make the next move.

'That's better,' he said, leaning back in his chair. 'Now, why don't you sit down?'

'Thank you – we'll stand,' said John.

'Please yourself,' said the colonel. He picked up the gold pencil on his blotter and turned it slowly for a moment before going on.

'First I want to assure you that the child Arlon is perfectly safe and in good hands.'

'He'd better be,' said Stephen.

'We have no desire to keep him here on Earth any longer than is necessary,' the colonel continued, ignoring the remark.

'Then give him to us and we'll get him back home,' said John.

'You'll get him home?'

The colonel's eyebrows rose. The pencil remained still between his fingers.

'Yes,' said John.

'But, my dear fellow, how do you propose to do that?'

Colonel M spoke evenly, as though explaining some unforeseen obstacle to a junior officer.

'We have means of getting back,' said John. He wondered whether Colonel M still believed that they, too, had come from Arlon's planet.

'Come, come. Are you telling me that you can return – all five of you – without a space-ship?'

John knew that he could push his bluff no further. Colonel M was well aware that Arlon could not jaunt. Probably, he had also guessed that the

Tomorrow People could not jaunt far without proper apparatus.

'Give us the space-ship, then we'll all go,' said Stephen.

'We shall be delighted to do so – once you have told us who you are and why you came here.'

The colonel paused, then added slowly, 'And after you have shown us how the space-ship works.'

There was silence for a moment. Then John spoke.

'We don't know how it works.'

Colonel M's teeth bared in another mirthless smile.

'You don't really expect me to believe that?' he said.

'It's true,' said Stephen.

'You are saying,' said Colonel M, 'that you travelled here, across many light-years of space in a ship that you don't know how to work?'

'We can drive it,' said Stephen. 'But we don't know anything about the engine. We're not engineers.'

'Even if that is so,' replied Colonel M, 'you must have some knowledge of its mechanism, otherwise you could hardly have brought it here. And my guess is that you know quite a lot more than you are prepared to admit. There are plenty of Earth boys of the ages you have chosen to impersonate who could explain how a liquid fuel rocket works. I am sure you can explain the basic principles of your space ship even if you really are children.'

There was another pause. John and Stephen dare not telepath to each other. They knew from their previous encounter that Colonel M himself possessed rudimentary telepathic powers. They could not run the risk of

83

his picking up their conversation. Finally, it was John who broke the silence.

'Why is it so important to you to know how the ship works?' he asked.

Colonel M regarded him steadily.

'You came to our planet, uninvited,' he said. 'And we were powerless to stop you.'

'We came here by accident,' said John.

'That may be,' replied the colonel. 'But if you who are only children can drop on us out of the skies, then who will come after you? Next time it may be an army, bent on destroying us, or reducing us to slavery.'

'We are a peaceful people,' said Stephen. 'We never attack anyone unless we are attacked first.'

'It is not merely you and your race whom we have to fear,' said Colonel M. 'Who knows what kind of people lurk out there in space, looking for new planets to conquer?'

'Very few people on other planets are like that,' said Stephen. 'Most of them gave up fighting wars millions of years ago.'

'Yet you yourselves, young though you are, have some pretty warlike weapons,' retorted Colonel M, pointing to the stun guns at their belts. 'And what is more, you know how to use them.'

The two boys remained silent, lost for an answer. They could not tell Colonel M that because they were Tomorrow People they could never kill any living thing.

'By coming here as you did,' continued Colonel M, 'you have taught us how badly we need an inter-planetary defence system. That's why we cannot let you go until we are sure that we can build a space-ship like yours.'

John wanted to argue, but he knew that it would be useless. No doubt Colonel M had genuinely convinced himself that the space-ships, once the Saps got them, would be used only for defence. The Tomorrow People knew differently, but they would never persuade a man like Colonel M.

'If we do try to do what you demand, will you release Arlon?' he asked.

'Of course,' replied Colonel M.

John looked at Stephen. Clearly, this was a problem for TIM.

'We'd like time to consider,' he told the Colonel.

'As long as you like,' said Colonel M. 'I'm sure you'll quickly realize that your best course is to cooperate.'

Bending over his papers once more, he did not even flicker an eyelid as John and Stephen jaunted back to the lab.

CHAPTER TEN

'It isn't an easy situation,' said John, 'but we have made one important gain. We now have access to the life-ship. What's more, we can go and examine it at our leisure, without having to paralyse everybody in sight. The Saps are only too eager to let us.'

'That's all very well,' protested Stephen. 'But they are expecting us to show them how it works.'

'We'll go back to Colonel M,' said John. 'We'll make him prove that Arlon is safe. Then we'll tell him that we accept his proposal, and let him take us to the life-ship. Once we have examined the engine, we should be able to see whether or not it is in working order.'

They knew that TIM, once he had the necessary data, would be able to give them a crash-course on the technology of the space-vehicle.

'One request from me,' put in TIM. 'Please pay

special attention to the computer inside the ship. You remember, it was being driven by a computer when it landed. I need to know whether it is programmed to return automatically to Crito.'

Since the Tomorrow People were now to be the Saps' guests, there was no need for anyone to be left behind at the lab. Accordingly, when Colonel M looked up from his papers once again, it was to see all four of them standing before him.

'A full turn-out this time,' he observed, with his iciest smile. 'May I take it that you have reached a sensible decision?'

'We'll show you how the space-ship works,' said Stephen. 'But we want Arlon first.'

'I'm afraid that's quite impossible,' said the colonel. 'I'm sure I need not explain why.'

'If you won't let us have him, at least let us see him,' John demanded. 'Then we'll know he's all right.'

'We've been trying to telepath to him but we can't,' put in Kenny. 'Something must be wrong.'

'Ah yes,' said the colonel. 'I'm afraid we had to drug him rather heavily to prevent his signalling his whereabouts. That was when we were transporting him, of course.'

'And now?' said John.

'I'm sure he should be awake,' replied the colonel. 'Why not try giving him a call?'

Cautiously, John telepathed to Arlon.

Back came the reply immediately, so joyful and excited that John would have been knocked unconscious once again had he not taken the precaution of throwing up a thought-screen.

88

'Try to tell us where you are,' Carol called.

Looking at the colonel's fixed smile, she wondered if he had picked up the question and knew it to be futile.

In any event, the answer did not reveal anything that would help them. Arlon sent back a confused picture of green lawns, a large room equipped with picture-books and toys, a matronly army nurse and a number of officers, some of them high-ranking, trying hard to play at uncle. But there was not the faintest clue which might tell them where the child was being held.

'It's no use trying to guess where he is,' said Colonel M. 'But as you see, he is safe and well.'

The Tomorrow People looked at one another. For the moment, it seemed, Colonel M had the upper hand. John turned to the colonel once more.

'Very well,' he said. 'We'll trust you. Take us to the space-ship.'

Two hours later, the colonel's helicopter touched down in a heavily-guarded field on the shores of Holy Loch. A few yards away stood the hangar in which the life-ship stood waiting.

Inside the hangar the experts were assembled, waiting for their lesson in astro-engineering. As the Tomorrow People entered a hush fell on the gathering. The American general's cigar remained rigid in the corner of his mouth and a French scientist stopped in mid-sentence, his outstretched hands falling limply to his sides.

So keen was the scrutiny focused upon them, that they each felt as though they were under a blaze of spotlights.

Towards the nose of the ship a section of the body had been removed and the superluminary engine stood exposed. Stephen, the technologist of the Tomorrow People, had been deputed to do the talking, and now it was he who stepped forward to examine it.

By any standards, the engine was an undoubted masterpiece; the work of some Criton genius who had succeeded in multiplying astro-energy units to a fantastic level, while reducing the number of components to the barest minimum. This had made the life-ship much lighter than other vehicles of its kind and enabled it to make the long journey to Earth without burning up its engine.

Stephen knew that it was beyond him to give a detailed explanation of the engine's workings, but he did at least understand the basic principles of superluminary flight, and these he now proceeded to expound. As he talked, he could see growing bewilderment on every face. They may be brilliant Saps, Stephen told himself, but they are still Saps.

While he was speaking, he was absorbing and memorizing every detail of the engine, ready for the escape-plan which TIM clearly had in mind. John, meanwhile, was photographing it from all angles with a miniature X-ray camera which he wore, disguised as a badge, in the lapel of his blazer.

'A ship of this kind may be manually operated,' Stephen told his hearers, 'but more usually, it is driven by a computer housed in the nose. I suggest that we now go inside the ship and have a look at that.'

The computer was certainly an impressive piece of work, but it was not to be compared with TIM. In that department, at least, the Critons were well behind the

Tomorrow People. A swift glance told Stephen that it was not programmed for a return to Crito.

Finally, Colonel M stepped forward.

'I am sure we are all more than grateful to our young friend for his exposition,' he said. 'Now, perhaps, he might be prepared to follow it up with a practical demonstration.'

For a moment, Stephen was completely taken aback.

'You surely don't mean that you want me to take you up for a flight?' he asked.

'Of course not,' said Colonel M. 'But if you were to show us how the controls work, and then rev up the engine, it might help to make your lecture a great deal clearer to us all.'

This demand was totally unexpected. For a moment Stephen was stumped. Walking slowly but thinking rapidly, he went to the front of the life-ship and examined the engine once more. 'I'm afraid I can't rev that,' he said. 'It's broken.'

'Broken?' Colonel M's eyes seemed to bore into his head.

Stephen indicated a curiously-shaped plate, made from a metal vastly harder than any diamond found on Earth. Roughly triangular, it was corrugated in an irregular pattern: for what reason, Stephen did not know.

'That plate,' he said. 'It's buckled. It must have happened when the ship hit the sea-bed.'

'Then we'll straighten it,' said Colonel M.

'I'm afraid you can't,' said Stephen. 'There aren't any tools on Earth strong enough to do the job.'

'Then how do you propose to return home, once we are ready to let you go?'

'We'll have to send to Crito for the necessary equipment,' replied Stephen.

'Send to Crito?' replied the Colonel, with a frown. 'How do you propose to do that?'

Stephen was stumped for a reply, but John was ready.

'It is a problem,' he told the colonel. 'I think, if you'll excuse us, that we had better go away and think about it. I'm sure we'll come up with something.'

Then, to the astonishment of the assembled experts, they jaunted out of sight. In a fifth of a second, they were back in the lab.

CHAPTER ELEVEN

'Well, that's settled one thing,' said TIM. 'The life-ship is in excellent working order.'

He had carefully examined the photographs and the other data which the Tomorrow People had brought back with them from Holy Loch.

'The Saps think it's broken,' said Carol.

'All the better,' declared John.

'What do you mean, John?' asked Kenny, with a puzzled frown.

'I mean that the life-ship will be able to take off when the Saps are least expecting it,' said John. 'And if everything goes according to plan, Arlon will be on board.'

Stephen, however, was worried. 'I've told the Saps that we need special equipment to repair the ship,' he pointed out. 'They are expecting me to get in touch with Crito.'

'Excellent,' said John. 'That's just what we are going to do.'

'But how?' asked Kenny. 'We don't know where it is.'

'We know that the Critons are a strongly telepathic race,' John told them, 'and if we can find some way of projecting our thoughts into deep space, in their general direction, there's a good chance that they will pick them up.'

'That's fine,' objected Stephen, 'except that we haven't got any equipment that will project thoughts across that sort of distance.'

'You're forgetting,' said John, 'there's a communicator in the life-ship.'

First, though, the proposal had to be put to Colonel M. Jaunting back to Loch Derrig, John told him that they had tried and failed to contact Crito, and that they would need the use of the life-ship communicator if they were to obtain the tools they needed.

For a moment, the colonel regarded him through his hard blue eyes, and once again John thought that he saw suspicion lurking there.

'Suppose I were to allow you to use it, how would the tools be sent?' he asked.

'Possibly by unmanned spacecraft,' replied John. 'Though we may need an engineer from Crito as well.'

'You mean, you don't think that you can carry out the repair by yourselves?'

'We told you, we are not engineers,' said John. 'We'll need advice from the experts on Crito, quite apart from the tools. We'll have a better idea when we have talked to them whether we can manage on our own, or whether somebody will have to come out to help us.'

The colonel pondered, twirling his gold pencil. Straining to pick up his thoughts, John felt even more certain that Colonel M suspected their motives. Finally, he looked at John squarely again.

'You realize that I can't hand over the communicator to you just like that?' he said.

'Of course,' replied John.

'It will require government approval at the very highest level. Indeed, the Prime Minister himself will have the final say in the matter.'

'If he wants to see the space-ship in working order, he'll say yes,' said John.

'Very well,' said Colonel M, finally. 'I'll contact Downing Street at once. I should have an answer for you in twelve hours.'

CHAPTER TWELVE

The pencil shape of the life-ship stood out starkly against the evening sky as Colonel M's helicopter swept low over the dark waters of the loch and came to rest outside the hangar. Swiftly, Colonel M climbed out, followed by Carol, John, Kenny and finally by Stephen. The security precautions were even greater than they had been before. A tight ring of military police guarded all the approach-roads, and this time there was no audience of scientific experts. They climbed into the life-ship and made their way to the nose where the communicator stood. It was essentially a larger and more powerful version of the ones the Tomorrow People used themselves, able to concentrate their telepathic thoughts and transmit them instantaneously across the light years of space.

Focusing his thoughts firmly into the communicator,

John telepathed a brief message. It informed the planet Crito that four young people on earth had urgent information about Arlon, son of the space-captain Saav.

Radio waves would have taken thousands of years to radiate out from Earth. John's thought message slipping through the intermedium of hyperspace flooded instantly to every part of the galaxy.

From time to time they glanced at Colonel M. Was he able to pick up what they were saying? For a time, it was hard to tell, but slowly they became convinced that he still believed them to be Critons.

For three hours they tried to make contact, the four of them taking turns. There was no response. By this time, they were all extremely tired.

'It's no use,' said John at last. 'We can't get through.'

'Have a rest, then try again,' suggested Colonel M.

The three older Tomorrow People stood at the window of the life-ship, staring moodily at the loch outside. It seemed as though the experiment had failed. Suddenly, Kenny, who had wandered back to the communicator, began to dance up and down.

'I've got someone!' he yelled gleefully. 'Somebody's answering – listen!'

John shot across the room and took Kenny's place.

Across millions of light-years, the answering signal came, faint but unmistakable.

'Calling Earth,' it said. 'Calling Earth. This is the planet Goros, acknowledging your call to Crito. Your signal is too weak to be received there, but we will relay your message.'

The Tomorrow People were almost too excited to

breathe. Goros was new to them, but clearly its inhabitants were a friendly and civilized race.

'Thank you, Goros,' John transmitted. 'Please tell Captain Saav, of the Criton space fleet, that his son Arlon has landed safely on Earth. We are endeavouring to return him, but will require precise navigational details so that his life-ship's computer can be programmed for the journey.'

After a brief delay, Goros informed the Tomorrow People that their message had been forwarded and that an overjoyed Captain Saav was flying there from Crito to speak to them directly. He was, added Goros, looking forward eagerly to a conversation with the son whom he had given up as totally lost.

The Tomorrow People looked at one another. How could they explain to Captain Saav that his son, though alive, was a prisoner?

Going to the far end of the ship for a moment, Carol swiftly called up TIM on her wrist-communicator. She told him what had happened.

Before TIM could reply, Kenny ran out to fetch her.

'Saav has come through,' he said.

CHAPTER THIRTEEN

If it hadn't been for their serious and intense expressions Colonel M might have thought that the four children were having him on.

They stood silent and expressionless while their minds reached out to make contact with an alien space captain thousands of miles away.

Colonel M pushed to the back of his own mind the worrying feeling that he could hear some of the children's silent conversation as they brought Saav up to date about what had happened.

'And so I'm afraid Arlon is still a prisoner of the Saps,' concluded John. 'We're extremely sorry to give you such bad news, but at least we can assure you that he is safe and well.'

For a moment, there was silence. At first, Saav had been delighted, then bewildered. Now his thought transmissions came as anger, harsh and unmistakable.

'What you have told me bears out all the ill reports which we have received of your planet,' said Saav, bitterly. 'When I heard that you had rescued my son and taken care of him, I was overwhelmed with gratitude and convinced that your nearer neighbours had slandered you. Now I know that they spoke the truth.'

'We are not all Saps – and not all Saps are evil,' protested John. 'Even the ones who are holding Arlon are not really bad men. They are just stupid and afraid.'

'And greedy and cruel,' declared Saav. 'Otherwise, how could they hold my little son as a hostage, merely in order to increase their own power?'

'They believe that they have to have space-ships like yours so that they can defend themselves against attack,' replied John.

'And who do they imagine would wish to attack their miserable Earth, with its wars, its poverty and its suicidal pollution?' demanded Saav. 'Believe me when I tell you that many planets have sent space-ships to study you, your broadcasts are monitored – you are subject to every kind of scrutiny. And what is the result? Everyone says that Earth is a disgrace to the universe – a place to steer clear of.'

'Things will be different when we take over,' said John. 'That's why nature has produced us. That's why we are Tomorrow People.'

'Forgive me,' Saav's thoughts softened. 'I should not speak to you in this way. Who knows what harm might have befallen Arlon at the hands of these Saps if you had not found him?'

'We are doing everything we can to get him back for you,' put in Carol, who had joined John at the communicator.

'I do not doubt it,' replied Saav. 'It is clear that you are risking your own lives in order to help him. And I am grateful, believe me.'

'If you can just be patient for a little longer . . .' urged Carol.

'No,' said Saav. 'I cannot take chances with the life of my son. Nor can I ask you to expose yourselves to further dangers. It is time that these Saps were taught a lesson.'

'But . . . what are you going to do?' asked John, his voice filled with anxiety.

'We shall send a punitive expedition to Earth,' said Saav. 'Of course, I shall require the approval of my government, but I do not doubt that it will be forthcoming. We shall demand the immediate return of Arlon, and if the Saps do not give him to us, we shall destroy them.'

The Tomorrow People turned pale with horror. That Saav meant what he said, they had not the slightest doubt. Unless they could find Arlon quickly and return him to his father, the whole Earth would find itself at war with a planet many times more powerful; a war which would bring disaster on a scale never even dreamed of.

'Have no fear for yourselves, my friends,' said Saav. 'We will, of course, ensure that you are safe. We will evacuate you to another planet; then, when the Saps are gone, you will be able to return.'

It was Carol who replied, her voice bold and clear.

'Saav,' she said, 'you have got to understand. Many of the Saps are all those things that you say they are; but many more are not. Our parents, our friends, are Saps. And in any case, no one can help being a Sap. They are just born that way.'

'If you destroy them all,' John cut in, 'you are just giving way to the kind of prejudice that causes wars and persecutions on Earth. You are blaming many people for the faults of a few.'

Stephen frowned. 'We want to take over the Earth,' he told Saav, 'but at the right time and in the right way. We don't want to do it over the Saps' dead bodies.'

'Please, Saav, don't kill the Saps,' begged Kenny. 'We'll get Arlon back for you – honestly we will.'

There was a long pause. Finally, Saav spoke again.

'Very well,' he said. 'I will wait for twelve of your Earth-hours before taking action. But if Arlon has not been released by then . . .'

The Tomorrow People did not wait for Saav to finish his sentence. Switching off the communicator, John turned to Colonel M.

'Are they sending the tools?' Colonel M asked.

'Tools nothing,' replied John. 'I've been speaking to Arlon's father. He says that if you don't release the child within twelve hours, the Criton forces are coming to destroy you.'

Once more Colonel M regarded him with his cold smile.

'Don't try to bluff me, laddie,' he said. 'I'm too old a hand to fall for that.'

John could see that to try to convince him would be

useless. He turned away, wondering desperately what they could do. Meanwhile, Carol had gone outside the room again to call up TIM on her communicator. She told him about Saav's ultimatum.

TIM's reply came back, calm and unperturbed.

'Don't worry about Saav, or about Colonel M. Come back to the lab – you've got work to do.'

'But TIM . . .' began Carol.

TIM cut her short.

'I've found Arlon.'

CHAPTER FOURTEEN

TIM had wasted no time in beginning his search for Arlon. Using a listening-device built into his system he had eavesdropped on the operation of every military computer in the land, until he had a complete picture of troop movements throughout the country. Sifting carefully through the mass of material, he soon discovered an exceptionally heavy concentration of military police and senior intelligence officers. The few clues which Arlon had telepathed clinched the matter: the little Criton was a prisoner at Tolford Grange.

As TIM programmed their belts for the rescue-jaunt, he warned the four Tomorrow People to be ultra-careful.

'Remember, the Saps will be on their guard,' he told them. 'And this time, you can't afford to make a mistake.'

107

Using aerial photographs taken from the observer satellite, TIM concluded that Arlon was almost certainly held in the security wing – an ugly brick section with barred windows and steel doors, normally used for interrogating spies. So finely did he programme their belts that they were scheduled to land right in the middle of the wing's upper storey, in the very room where Arlon was most likely to be found.

Finally, they were ready. John looked at his three companions. 'All set?' he asked.

The others nodded, trying hard not to show their nervousness.

'Right, TIM,' said John.

'Good luck,' said TIM. And with that, they jaunted.

CHAPTER FIFTEEN

They landed in the middle of a large, bleak room which
reminded them at once of Colonel M's office at Loch
Derrig. But there had been determined efforts to
brighten it: someone had hung nursery-rhyme pictures
round the walls and the floor was littered with toys.

At the far end of the room sat Arlon, chortling with
delight at a toy motor-car which the army nurse had set
running across the carpet. Incongruously, Kenny found
himself wondering whether they had motor-cars on
Crito.

Arlon had his back to them and the nurse saw them
first. As she started to scream, Kenny gave her a squirt
from his stun gun. She remained motionless, her mouth
open. Arlon turned and greeted them with a squeal
which they felt even through their thought-screens.

John and Stephen spun round to see two military

109

policemen, stationed beside the door, reaching for their pistols. Two stun guns spurted and they, too, froze rigid.

'Come on, Arlon,' said Carol, taking his hand. 'Let's get out of here.'

Swiftly they stole out into a short, draughty corridor, where two more sentries patrolled up and down. On hearing the door open, one of them had stepped up to investigate. As Stephen dealt with him, John sprang forward to paralyse his comrade.

In front of them, at the end of the corridor, stood a tiny lift with its gates open.

'In here,' said John, bundling Carol and Arlon in front of him. It was a tight squeeze for five of them, but they just managed it.

At the ground floor entrance, they would be sure to find more sentries. John and Stephen pressed the tips of their stun guns through the lift-gates, ready to squirt at the sight of a red cap. But they were not to get the chance.

No sooner had the lift passed the first floor than there was a shout and a rush of feet, and the lift stopped.

'They've switched the power off!' yelled Stephen. 'We're trapped!'

He was right. Discovering their paralysed comrades on the second floor, the redcaps had rushed to stop the lift and were now massing to deal with the Tomorrow People.

John thought swiftly. They could not see the ground floor, so to jaunt there was a risk. However, there seemed to be no alternative.

'Right, Kenny,' he said. 'Just the two of us. Jaunt!'

He knew that if he and Kenny went astray, Stephen would be needed to get Carol and Arlon out of the mess somehow.

A fifth of a second later they landed – bang on target, behind a bunch of redcaps who were massing by the lift gates.

An officer was directing operations.

'Sergeant,' he rapped, 'take six men and cover them from the first floor. Shoot if you have to, but try to avoid . . .'

He never finished the sentence. Using their stun guns like blow-lamps, John and Kenny paralysed the lot of them before they could turn round.

While Kenny covered the entrance, John dived into the basement to search for the master-switch which would set the lift going again. Wrenching open a cupboard, he found himself facing a battery of switches. One, undoubtedly, was the switch he needed, but there was nothing to indicate which it was.

John hesitated, but only for a second. Using the flat of his hand, he flicked the switches down in rows; within seconds, a shout from above told him that the lift was moving once more.

By interfering with the switchboard, John had stopped lifts and set fans whirring in all parts of the building. As they raced out of the door into the sunlight, more redcaps came running from other doors.

While John and Stephen faced them with their stun guns, Kenny and Carol raced across the wide lawn to the helicopter which they knew was kept there.

The leading redcaps reached for their holsters, but John stunned them with a couple of quick bursts. The others hesitated, fearful of coming on. At the edge of the lawn, the helicopter roared, its propeller revved into life and it rose slowly into the air.

The braver redcaps moved forward and then stopped, their jaws hanging open. For John and Stephen had disappeared. They had jaunted, safely into the helicopter.

CHAPTER SIXTEEN

As soon as he heard of Arlon's escape, the Prime Minister summoned an urgent meeting of the Cabinet. The Minister of Defence, normally an urbane man, looked harassed and unhappy.

'According to my latest information, Prime Minister, the helicopter is now nearing the Scottish border,' he said. 'It should be at Holy Loch within the hour.'

'Where the army and navy have obligingly prepared the space-ship for immediate lift-off,' observed the Prime Minister icily.

'We were anticipating a practical demonstration . . .' began the Minister of Defence.

'And you are undoubtedly going to receive one,' the Prime Minister interrupted, 'though it won't be quite the sort of demonstration you had in mind. These young people will simply fly off to Crito and that is the last that we shall see of them. Unless, of course, you can think of something to prevent it.'

Colonel M, meanwhile, had already arrived back at the Holy Loch. He stood beside the life-ship, lost in thought, while the captain, who had come from Loch Derrig, stamped up and down impatiently.

'I wish you'd stop that,' snapped the colonel, raising his head. 'It's not helping matters a bit.'

The captain drew a deep breath.

'Sir,' he said, 'I want to ask why we don't just shoot them down. We could do it so easily.'

'Shoot them down,' repeated the colonel, with cold disdain. 'Five kids, just like that. Suppose one of them was your kid, would you want to shoot them down then?'

'But look what they have done,' protested the captain.

'They have done nothing,' said Colonel M, 'except defend themselves – and that they have done with extraordinary courage and determination. Yet from start to finish, they have not shed a drop of blood. I have been ordered not to shed theirs, and that order I shall obey.'

'Even though they have made us look silly fools?' ventured the captain.

'Perhaps that's exactly what we are,' responded Colonel M, broodingly.

The captain looked at his superior officer in astonishment.

'I don't understand, sir,' he said.

'If these youngsters are telling the truth – and I believe now that they may be – they are at this very moment in the process of trying to save us all from destruction,' said Colonel M.

'You think the Critons really are preparing to attack us?' asked the captain.

'Consider what the youngsters can do,' Colonel M told him. 'They can appear and disappear at will. They can project and receive thoughts. They have fantastic technological skill and weapons that leave us powerless, though unharmed.'

'But, sir . . .' began the captain. The colonel cut him short.

'If they had not outwitted us once again, I might have been ready to go on with the battle,' he said. 'But if youngsters of their age are so powerful, what must the professional soldiers of Crito be like? I'm beginning to think that we were mad ever to risk a visit from their space-fleet.'

'So we're just going to let them go?' asked the captain.

'No,' replied Colonel M. 'When they arrive, we'll have one last try. But this time, it will be persuasion – not force.'

At that moment, they heard a low hum in the distance. The colonel strained his eyes.

'Looks as though they are here,' he said.

The hum became a roar and the roar an enormous clatter as the helicopter swept low over the mountains and landed. Swiftly the Tomorrow People stepped out, stun guns at the ready. They made a protective shield around Arlon, who beamed with delight as he saw his life-ship once more.

Colonel M stepped forward.

'You can put those away,' he said. 'We shall not attempt to use any kind of force to detain you here.'

The Tomorrow People did not move.

'We could have shot you down,' said the colonel gently. 'We could have picked you off with a rifle as you stepped out of the plane. Or, indeed, we could have put the space-ship back in its hangar.'

Slowly, the Tomorrow People put their stun guns in their holsters.

'I want to make one last appeal,' said Colonel M. 'You come from a planet infinitely more advanced than ours – advanced in technology and, perhaps, in other branches of knowledge also.'

The Tomorrow People waited.

'Pass on some of that knowledge to us, before you depart,' asked Colonel M, humbly.

John shook his head.

'I'm sorry,' he said. 'One day, perhaps sooner than you think, the people of Earth will possess the knowledge that you are asking for. But you are not ready yet.'

Taking Arlon by the hand, he turned and walked towards the life-ship, the others following. Colonel M watched them for a moment; then, with a sad shake of the head, he walked slowly away. Behind him went the captain, a bewildered expression on his weak-chinned face.

At that moment, another hum was heard in the distance, this time from the direction of the road. The Tomorrow People turned and stared. Slowly, round a bend at the foot of the mountains, came two tiny figures on motor-bikes. In a few minutes they had roared to a stop and were racing across the field towards the life-ship, past guards too astonished to stop them.

Arlon's face broke into a big grin and he waved excitedly.

'It's Ginge and Lefty!' cried Carol in astonishment.

'Just in time,' panted Ginge, as he reached them.

Lefty, equally breathless, had a grin to match Arlon's.

When he had recovered, Ginge told them: 'We knew you'd come here as soon as you'd cracked it – and it looks as though you have.'

'I'll only feel sure about that,' said John, 'once Arlon is safely on his way.'

Ginge smiled at Arlon.

'Lefty's got something for you,' he said.

Unhooking an authentic Hell's Angel badge from his belt, Lefty presented it to the child.

'That's to remind you of us when you get back home,' said Ginge.

Arlon looked at the badge for a long moment. Then, carefully fastening it to his tunic, he held out his hand to the two Hell's Angels before climbing up to the door of the ship. There he smiled and waved a final farewell.

'You lot going too, then?' Ginge asked John, who had waited at the top of the steps.

John gave him a wink.

'Remember, we're still Critons,' he said in a low voice.

With help from Goros, TIM had already programmed the life-ship's computer by remote control. As Arlon took a last look at the Earth's landscape, Stephen began the lift-off procedures. In seconds, the ship was zooming out towards the stars.

'Well, this is where we get off, Arlon,' John told the little boy.

'Thank you, my dear friends,' Arlon replied, taking their hands in turn. 'I shall never forget you.'

Carol embraced him, then the four jaunted.

On the ground, Colonel M was staring upwards towards the life-ship, now a rapidly disappearing dot of light in the darkening sky.

'It's a tremendous pity,' he said to the captain. 'Indeed it's a tragedy. Only think what we might have learned from them.'

Even as he spoke, far below the London streets, the Tomorrow People arrived back in their laboratory.

Roger Price
The Tomorrow People in **Three in Three** 40p

The professor who has the secret of total destruction . . .

The Great Mothers of Matra, giant women who live for ever . . .

The evil Guru Jedikiah, whose power matches that of the Tomorrow
People themselves . . .

Three exciting adventures which take the Tomorrow People from
Scotland to strange and distant planets, and back to California.

The Tomorrow People in **Four into Three** 40p

In this book the Tomorrow People are joined by Tyso, a young gypsy
boy, in three more thrilling adventures in which they encounter:

The warlike Kraatans, whose one aim is to invade the Earth . . .

The Aliens, who appear suddenly in the lab and set the Tomorrow
People against each other . . .

And the villainous Kleptons, whose monstrous greed and cruelty bring
them harsh punishment.

The Tomorrow People in
The Lost Gods with **Hitler's Last Secret** and
The Thargon Menace 70p

A glider crash brings Mike and John to an Oriental temple where they
discover a new Tomorrow Person . . . the Tomorrow People battle a
gang of Nazis whose eternal youth is Hitler's last and most evil secret
weapon . . . and they have to decide whether the occupants of the
Thargon space ship which crashes to the Earth are the refugees they
claim to be – or are they something much more sinister?

Judy Blume
Then Again, Maybe I Won't 70p

Tony is thirteen and he's just moved house. Now he lives in the best
part of Long Island, surrounded by luxury homes and swimming pools.
Next door there's Joel who's a dab hand at shoplifting. Joel's older
sister Lisa gets undressed every night with the lights on and the curtains
open. Tony's mother thinks everything's swell on Long Island. She wants
Tony to be just like the kids next door – or does she?

It's Not the End of the World 70p

Karen is twelve and her world is crumbling. First of all her mother and
father were arguing all the time – then her father moved out and didn't
come back. Now he's going to Las Vegas to fix up a divorce. Karen's new
friend Val has been through it too . . . But maybe Karen and her brother
Jeff and baby sister Amy can somehow stop it happening – or maybe
they just don't stand a chance.

Catherine Cookson
Go Tell It to Mrs Golightly 70p

Despite everything, Bella was a brave and cheerful girl. Her father was a
drunk, disowned by the family, and she had had to learn to live with her
sightless eyes. Sometimes she must have thought that Mrs Golightly
was the only friend she had in the world – even when everyone said that
the old woman was a figment of Bella's imagination; but she was going
to need Mrs Golightly, especially when real danger arrived like a bolt
from the blue . . .

Nina Beachcroft
Under the Enchanter 60p

The Hearsts are an ordinary family who rent an ordinary Yorkshire farmhouse for their holiday. But soon Laura and her brother Andrew discover something very out of the ordinary . . . above the stables there lives an elderly man – the malevolent and smiling Mr Strange. Laura is wary, but Andrew likes him. Then Andrew begins to change, drifting into a weird dreamworld . . .

Mollie Hunter
The Ghosts of Glencoe 75p

Amidst the thick snows of February, under the shadow of the great mountains of Glencoe, the red-coated soldiers came in the dead of night . . . They had their orders – to turn on the homes of the Macdonalds and slaughter every man, woman and child. It was one of the most infamous and brutal massacres in history. For Robert Stewart, the young red-coat officer, it meant a fearsome choice – between carrying out his orders and abandoning his military ambitions in a desperate attempt to save the doomed clansmen . . .